His kiss was slow, deliberate and provocative.

Masterful. His lips were soft but insistent. Surprisingly seductive. He tasted of rich, honeyed darkness, of mystery. The musky male scent of heat and spice clouded her bemused brain.

Alissa's eyes widened as she registered pleasure at his skilful caress. A tiny spark of feminine appreciation. A rippling tide of awareness that heated her blood.

Ruthlessly she crushed it, ignoring too the sizzle of unexpected pleasure as his hands all but spanned her waist, making her feel dainty, feminine and delicate.

Desperately she focussed on pushing him away. Yet her efforts had no effect. He swamped her senses till she was aware of nothing but his hot, heady presence, and the undertow of desire threatening to drag her under. A slow-turning twist of unfamiliar tension coiled deep inside her.

Eventually he lifted h
dumbfounded, at t
husband. She hadn't
More, she couldn't b
so...disturbing. How could she
to a man she didn't want?

Annie West spent her childhood with her nose between the covers of a book—a habit she retains. After years of preparing government reports and official correspondence she decided to write something she *really* enjoys. And there's nothing she loves more than a great romance. Despite her office-bound past, she has managed a few interesting moments—including a marriage offer with the promise of a herd of camels to sweeten the contract. She is happily married to her ever-patient husband (who has never owned a dromedary). They live with their two children amongst the tall eucalypts at beautiful Lake Macquarie, on Australia's east coast. You can e-mail Annie at www.annie-west.com, or write to her at PO Box 1041, Warners Bay, NSW 2282, Australia.

Recent books by the same author:

THE DESERT KING'S PREGNANT BRIDE
THE GREEK TYCOON'S UNEXPECTED WIFE

BLACKMAILED BRIDE, INNOCENT WIFE

BY
ANNIE WEST

MILLS & BOON®
Pure reading pleasure™

All the characters in this book have no existence outside the imagination
of the author, and have no relation whatsoever to anyone bearing the
same name or names. They are not even distantly inspired by any
individual known or unknown to the author, and all the incidents are
pure invention.

First published in Great Britain 2009
Harlequin Mills & Boon Limited,
Eton House, 18-24 Paradise Road, Richmond, Surrey TW9 1SR

© Annie West 2009

ISBN: 978 0 263 87205 7

Set in Times Roman 10 on 11½ pt
01-0509-54162

Printed and bound in Spain
by Litografia Rosés, S.A., Barcelona

BLACKMAILED BRIDE, INNOCENT WIFE

To all the readers who have enjoyed my stories.

To the many who have taken the time
to contact me about my books.

And especially to Sofia, Cindy, Gena and Dottie,
who were the very first to encourage
a brand-new author on her debut.

Thank you all!

CHAPTER ONE

ALISSA stepped off the tram just as the leaden Melbourne sky opened, releasing a downpour. She had no umbrella. The weather had been the last thing on her mind today.

Thunder cracked so close she expected the pavement to shatter before her. The temperature plummeted. Alissa shivered, suddenly chilled to the marrow.

It's a sign, an omen.

She grimaced, refusing to heed the superstitious inner voice. The voice of foreboding that had plagued her all day. The storm had been predicted days ago. It wasn't an omen of disaster. It was mere coincidence.

Alissa ignored the way the hairs on her neck prickled. She hunched her shoulders and darted along the pavement, heedless of the rain's drenching needles.

She'd planned this afternoon meticulously. Nothing, not a storm or her own doubts, would stop her when so much was at stake. Success was so close.

All she had to do was…marry.

Her pace faltered as her heel jammed against uneven pavement. She was doing the right thing, the *only* thing she could. Yet fear slid like an icy finger down her spine at the idea of marriage.

Tying herself to a man.

It didn't matter that this wedding was her idea. That Jason was unthreatening. Safe. Or that the marriage would be short-lived. Experience had taught her the danger of being in a man's power. All the logic in the world couldn't stop the atavistic dread freezing her veins.

But this was no time for caution. Donna needed her. This was her sister's last chance.

Alissa would do *anything*, even tackle her darkest terrors, to save her beloved sister. No one else could do this. The burden rested on her shoulders.

Setting her jaw, she climbed the steps of the looming public building. One leaden foot in front of the other.

It will be all right…unbidden, the old mantra filled her mind.

Of course it would be all right. She and Jason would marry and after six months they'd go their separate ways, unencumbered but for the money they'd receive. The money that would save Donna's life.

It was a simple business arrangement. No power play. No threat. A win-win situation.

Nothing could go wrong.

She hurried through the entrance, plunged into the gloomy foyer and tripped over something.

'Careful there!' an abrupt voice commanded.

Large hands grasped her elbows, holding her away from the solid body her momentum had flung her against. Heat encircled her, the smell of spicy, warm male skin and citrus aftershave. Alissa's pulse skittered at the understated yet unmistakable invitation of that heady scent.

She leaned away to see what she'd fallen over.

Shoes. Large enough to match the hands holding her so firmly. Glossy black handmade shoes that had never seen a scuff in their privileged life. The sight of that perfect footwear, of elegant suiting stretched over long, powerful legs, unsettled her as much as the stranger's silence.

She stepped back but his hands didn't fall. Annoyance skated through her.

Alissa raised her eyes. Past the exquisitely cut jacket, custom-made to accommodate broad shoulders and a rangy frame. Up to an angular jaw, scrupulously shaved. A firm mouth, wide and superbly sculpted, a slash of sensuality across an otherwise hard face. A long, decisive nose, bracketed by high cheekbones that gave him an aristocratic air of disdain.

The air hissed through Alissa's teeth as she drew a sharp breath. His face was lean, harsh, arrogant. With his black hair combed back from a widow's peak he looked impossibly elegant. But his eyes... Alissa reeled as she stared into a charcoal gaze ripe with disapproval.

Heaven help the woman he'd come here to marry.

With those looks—male model meets pure testosterone—his bride was probably too besotted to realise what she was in for. But one moment's collision with his piercing, censorious gaze told Alissa everything. He had an ego big enough to match those shoes. More, there was danger in his superior look, his air of latent power.

Trouble. That was what he was. Why any woman would shackle herself to a man like that...

'I'm sorry,' she muttered when she got her tongue to move. 'I was in such a hurry to get out of the rain I didn't see you there.'

Silence.

His brows arrowed down in a V of displeasure.

Alissa lifted a hand to her soaked hair. A dribble of rain slid down her nape. Her suit clung to her breasts, back and legs. Even her toes were damp. She shivered as cold sliced through her.

What was wrong with him? Did he disapprove of the way she looked? Or the fact that she'd run into him?

Uncontrollable, unladylike little hoyden. The words rang so loud and clear Alissa jumped. But it was her grandfather's hoarse voice she heard. The stranger's cold gaze had evoked an unexpected memory. The realisation shook her to the core. She must be even more nervous than she'd realised to hear the old man from the grave.

'Look, I—'

'Do you usually burst through doors like that? Without looking where you're going?' His voice was low, deep, with a husky edge that made her skin prickle, but not with fear or cold this time. It was a bedroom voice, made for seducing women to mindless compliance. A slight accent lengthened the vowels, producing a tantalising drawl. To her annoyance, she felt the zap and tingle of nerves reacting to the masculine timbre of that voice.

'I didn't burst anywhere.' She stood straighter, yanking her arms free. To her chagrin she barely reached his shoulder. Typical! That excess height no doubt added to his belief in his own superiority.

Those frowning brows rose in supercilious disbelief. He'd probably never been caught without an immaculately cut raincoat, or perhaps a lackey hovering with an umbrella.

'My apologies for interrupting your…reverie. I'll leave you in peace.'

Alissa spun round and strode away. She felt his glare graze the bare skin of her neck and the sway of her hips as she shortened her stride to accommodate her heels.

But she didn't mistake his stare for male admiration.

His regard was contemptuous, sharp as a blade. Why, she had no idea. But she had enough experience of disapproving men to recognise his animosity.

Perhaps his fiancée was late and he wasn't used to waiting so he'd taken out his impatience on her.

Alissa tilted her chin and stepped through a doorway into the corridor she needed. She had a marriage to attend and no time for speculating over strangers.

'He said *what*?' Her voice rose in breathless disbelief. Alissa shook her head, wondering if the soaking had somehow affected her hearing.

The clerk shrugged and spread his hands. 'That he couldn't make the appointment.'

The appointment! Alissa stared, numb with shock, hearing the loud thrum of her pulse in the silence. This was hardly an *appointment*. This was a *wedding*. Jason's wedding as well as hers. Was this a joke?

No, not a joke. Jason was as eager for this marriage as she. Well, as eager for the money they'd get when they inherited her grandfather's Sicilian estate then sold it. He'd jumped at the idea of a convenient wedding with an alacrity that surprised her. His need for cash was greater than she'd first thought.

Surely this was a mistake. Jason must be running late, that was all.

'What, exactly, did he say?' she asked through stiff lips.

The clerk darted a speculative glance at her before reading the note in his hand. 'Mr Donnelly rang thirty minutes ago and said he wouldn't be able to come. He'd changed his mind.'

Another sharply curious glance accompanied the words. Yet Alissa was beyond feeling embarrassed that her bridegroom had done a runner. The news was too devastating for humiliation even to register. This was disaster on a cataclysmic scale.

She linked her fingers tight together, willing herself to be calm. Her heart thudded out of control as panic edged her thoughts. Her stomach descended into freefall.

She couldn't afford to fail. The very idea knotted her stomach with dread.

What would she do if Jason really had jilted her?

Alissa *had* to marry. If within the next thirty-one days she wasn't Mrs Someone-or-other, married as required by the terms of her grandfather's will, she could kiss goodbye to the chance of getting Donna to the States for the treatment she needed.

Contesting the will would take too long and her solicitor had warned the outcome of such legal action wasn't certain. As for getting a loan to cover the astronomical costs…the banks had disabused her of that possibility. There were no other options but to do the one thing she'd vowed she never would—comply with her despised grandfather's last wishes in order to inherit part of his estate. The old so-and-so would be chortling in hell if he could see the fix she was in now.

She pinned a tight smile to her face and drew a slow, calming breath. 'Was there anything else?'

'No.' The clerk couldn't hide the inquisitive glimmer in his eyes. 'That was all.'

'I see. Thank you.' But she didn't see. This made no sense.

She turned away and drew out her cellphone. Punching in Jason's number with an unsteady hand, she lifted it to her ear, only to hear the infuriating engaged signal. Had something terrible happened or was he avoiding her? It took a moment to realise he could have phoned her instead of the marriage registry. So yes, he was avoiding her.

Alissa put a hand to her brow, flummoxed. What was she going to do? Panic edged her whirling thoughts. She'd go to Jason's, but she felt an unnerving certainty he wouldn't be at his flat or anywhere else she looked.

'Miss Scott?' The clerk's voice made her swing round eagerly. Had Jason turned up?

Hope died instantly. There was only the clerk and, with him, the tall stranger from the foyer.

Why was he here? She cast a swift glance at those narrowed eyes and looked away, feeling again that *frisson* of reaction to his blatant stare. The man made her supremely uncomfortable.

'Yes?' She stepped forward, concentrating on the clerk, not the stranger beside him.

'This gentleman is here to see you.'

'To see *me*?' She forced herself to look up into that beautiful, arrogant face and ignore the tremor of consternation that ran through her.

'If you are Miss Alissa Scott?'

She nodded. 'I am.'

'Affianced to Jason Donnelly?'

'That's right.' Her mouth dried. He had the deliberate, enigmatic tone of a judge pronouncing sentence.

'Granddaughter of Gianfranco Mangano?'

She nodded jerkily, her lips primming at the mention of her late, unlamented grandfather.

'We need to talk. I have news for you.'

'From Jason?' Was that why he'd been loitering in the foyer? To explain Jason's absence? Why hadn't he said so?

'*Si.*' The single word was curt, his expression sombre, and Alissa felt a presentiment of trouble, deep trouble.

He gestured for her to accompany him, not waiting to see if she complied before striding away. Alissa scurried to keep up, her feet sliding in her damp shoes.

He'd reached the foyer, heading for the main door, when she caught him up.

'Where are you going?'

He paused and turned his head, eyes narrowing on her. 'My limousine is outside. We can talk privately there.'

She shook her head. She was going nowhere with a man she didn't know. Especially not this man. Especially not into some anonymous vehicle. She was desperate, not a fool.

'We can talk here.' She angled her chin up.

'You wish to discuss your private affairs *here*, in such a public place?'

She met his gaze steadily. Better to err on the side of caution. 'You said you had news for me?'

Dario looked into that upturned oval face and felt it again— the stab of physical awareness. Despite everything, his hatred of the Mangano family, his contempt for this woman, his fury at the steps he'd been forced to take to secure what was his, there was no mistaking her impact on him. An intense jolt of

desire carved a hole right through his belly. Its burning trail was
hot as flame.

A similar, unexpected surge of need had held him still when
she'd run into him five minutes ago. He'd been stunned by its
intensity—far stronger even than his disgust.

This was the woman who'd rejected his offers, rejected *him*
not once but twice now, not even deigning to meet him in person.
That alone was an insult for which he required satisfaction. No
woman had ever denied him what he wanted. More, she connived
to thwart his plans to recoup what was his. She'd schemed behind
his back, collaborating with Donnelly to prevent Dario winning
back his birthright.

She wanted it all for herself. If she'd planned to marry for love
he might have understood. But this was a greedy, calculating
attempt to keep the old feud alive and stop him acquiring the one
thing that meant everything to him. The *castello* in Sicily her
grandfather had stolen from Dario's family.

He breathed deep, suppressing a lifetime's hatred.

This woman was everything he despised. Shallow, conniving,
spoiled. She'd grown up with every advantage money could buy
yet she'd squandered her opportunities, turning instead to drugs,
drink and wild parties. Till even her grandfather would have
nothing to do with her.

Dario should feel nothing but contempt for her. And yet…

Her pale, pure skin, her wide-open cornflower eyes, her plump
bow of a mouth, the voluptuous curves on that tiny figure…even
her air of barely suppressed energy, comprised a feminine
package that was far too alluring.

It infuriated him. It was not supposed to happen. And things
which were not supposed to happen had a way of disappearing
silently out of his life: bought off or simply banished by his
superior power and strength of will. Dario had worked hard for
what he had. He had no patience with things or people, or
feelings, that did not comply with his plans.

'What I have to say isn't for public consumption.'

He punched down irritation at her contrary attitude in refusing to accompany him. What had he expected? Her previous actions, having her lawyer reject his more than generous offers out of hand, illustrated her selfish obstinacy.

He drew a breath, trying to block the rich scent of lilies and damp woman that played havoc with his concentration.

'Come. Let us find a better place for this conversation.' He'd be damned if he discussed matters of such importance in an echoing public foyer. She might have few scruples but he had more respect for himself than that.

He stalked across the vestibule and found an empty office. He held the door and waited for her to precede him.

His gaze strayed down over her compact, curvaceous figure as she entered, the sway of her pert bottom in the tight skirt. Even in a rain-stained suit, with saturated hair, her complexion milky with shock, she drew his unwilling gaze.

Despite those top-class legs, reason dictated she wasn't his type. Pocket Venus redheads with attitude and tarnished reputations weren't his style. Give him a brunette with a madonna smile and a docile nature any day.

Unfortunately the voice of reason stayed silent on this occasion.

'What is this place?' She stared at the desk before them. 'Are we allowed in here?'

He shrugged and closed the door. 'We are here. And we have privacy. That's all that matters.'

Her eyes widened and she opened her mouth as if to argue then clearly thought better of it.

Good. Things would proceed more easily when she learned to accede to his wishes. A shaft of anticipation warmed his belly at the thought.

'Your bridegroom—'

'What happened to Jason? Have you seen him?' No mistaking the concern in her voice. He catalogued the fact for later consideration. Perhaps, after all, their wedding hadn't been purely a convenient arrangement. Perhaps lust as well as greed had been a factor in her marriage plans.

He remembered Jason Donnelly's weak, handsome face—good looks but no substance. Was he the sort of man that attracted her? The idea was strangely disquieting. He had no interest in this woman's weaknesses, except insofar as he could exploit them to his advantage.

'I saw him this afternoon.'

'Is he all right? What happened?'

Dario felt a stirring of pleasure, remembering the ease with which this afternoon's interview had followed the map he'd laid out for it.

'Nothing happened. Your Mr Donnelly is perfectly well, though he is no longer *your* Mr Donnelly.'

Her brow puckered in a frown and Dario wondered if he'd let his satisfaction show. What did it matter if he had? There was nothing she could do about it. He held all the cards. No matter how much she protested, she'd find the only way forward was *his* way. After all the trouble she'd caused the knowledge pleased him.

'I don't understand.'

'He has decided he no longer wishes to marry you.'

'But why? And why not tell me himself? Why send a stranger?'

'He didn't send me. I chose to come.'

Her eyes widened as she met his gaze. Then she sagged back against the desk, shaking her head.

'Look, can't you just tell me? What's going on?'

'Mr Donnelly had a better offer. An offer he found it impossible to refuse. As a result he changed his mind about marriage.' Dario had made absolutely sure of that.

'An offer of what? Not marriage!'

Dario paced further into the room to stand before her, his feet planted wide, his hands finding his pockets as he enjoyed this moment of triumph.

'An offer of money, of course. That's the language the two of you understand best.' He watched her pupils dilate, darkening her eyes. Her jaw sagged to reveal even white teeth and a glimpse of moist pink tongue.

Dario frowned. It was impossible that any woman should look sexy while gawping in disbelief, but somehow Alissa Mangano…no, Alissa Scott, managed it. That mouth was ripe, luscious, inviting. He felt a tingle of awareness, a tightening of muscles as his gaze zeroed in on the dainty curl of her tongue circling her lips.

He set his jaw. Lust for this woman was *not* on his agenda. His standards were higher than that.

'Money to do what?' She stood straight now, her momentary weakness sloughed. She stuck her hands on her hips, a picture of demanding femininity. Her neat chin jutted belligerently. 'And who made him this offer?'

Dario permitted himself a small, satisfied smile. 'I did. I offered him enough cash to ensure he gave up all thoughts of marrying you.'

It had been ludicrously easy. If Donnelly and this woman were lovers, there was no loyalty between them. Donnelly had jumped at the chance of cash in hand with no thought for the woman he'd jilt. It had been Dario who suggested he leave a message at the registry office.

Colour flagged her cheeks and her eyes sparked, giving her a vibrancy that had been missing before. A vibrancy that only enhanced her looks.

'Why would you do that?' She took a step closer as if to get a better look at him, staring straight into his eyes. Despite himself, Dario was impressed that she wasn't daunted as so many people were in his presence.

But then she didn't yet know who he was.

He shrugged and spread his hands. 'Because he was in the way.' And Dario had no patience for obstacles in his path. 'Because you will be marrying me instead.'

CHAPTER TWO

HE MEANT it!

Unbelievably this stranger was in deadly earnest. Alissa shivered and curled her arms tight round herself. She stared up into that smirking, satisfied, gorgeous face and felt the bottom drop out of her world.

'Who the devil *are* you?' It emerged as a hoarse whisper, barely audible despite the stillness of the room.

For a heartbeat, then two, then three, there was silence.

'I am Dario Parisi.'

The words echoed in her ears like a death knell. Why hadn't she guessed before? The Italian accent, the outrageously handsome face, the arrogance, the air of discreet elegance only serious money could achieve. *The hatred in his eyes.*

But who'd believe he'd cross the globe to confront her in person? He'd been persistent. Now it seemed he was obsessed.

Alissa bit her unsteady lip. Looking into the intense burn of that stare was like looking into the scorching fires of hell. Dangerous, unforgiving and inescapable. She already knew this man was without mercy or finer feeling.

He had a reputation for ruthlessness and success the Press adored. In business he was without rival, letting nothing stand in his way when he wanted something. And in love…he had a reputation for being just as ruthless in acquiring and discarding gorgeous women.

'I'm delighted you remember my name,' he drawled, the sting of sarcasm making her wince. 'I thought perhaps you'd put it from your mind.'

How could she when it had been imprinted on her consciousness every day? Her grandfather had been determined to marry her to Dario Parisi, alternately extolling his virtues and threatening her with retribution if she didn't obey. He'd taken special delight in reading out reports in the Italian papers describing Parisi's phenomenal success and his merciless tactics.

Her shivers grew to a shudder. A huge spider seemed to tap-dance down her backbone. She gritted her teeth and stood straighter, willing the trembling to recede.

It didn't matter how powerful he was, or that years of threats had turned Dario Parisi into a name to fear. He was just a man. Wealthy, ruthless, determined, but he had no power over her.

'You could have told me your name straight away. Or didn't it suit your desire for melodrama?' She refused to look away from that accusing glare. 'Was I supposed to faint at the realisation I was in your presence?'

Alissa wouldn't let him see how close she'd been to doing precisely that. Her heart pumped double time and her body was rigid from an overdose of adrenalin. But she had to stand up to him. She'd learned that was the only way to deal with a bully.

He scowled and Alissa experienced a fillip of delight that she'd chipped his superior air.

'But then,' he said in an easy voice as if she hadn't spoken, 'it's not surprising you remember the name of the man you were supposed to marry.'

'We were never—'

'Ah, but we were, Alissa.' He spoke her name like a slow, lethal caress, his emphasis on the sibilants giving it a whole new, provocative sound. 'It had been agreed.' The heat left his eyes, replaced by chilly hauteur.

'Not by me!' She drew herself up to her full height, glaring unabashed into his dark stare. 'Surely the bride has something to say in such circumstances.'

He shrugged those broad shoulders in a movement that was pure Italian male. She hated it.

'Not necessarily,' he murmured.

She stared.

Not necessarily.

That attitude summed him up. He was just like the old man: manipulative, domineering and chauvinistic. Yet he was only in his early thirties. What was it about Sicily that produced men like that, all ego and testosterone?

'In this century women have as much say in who they marry as men. And I didn't want to marry you.'

Shards of ice rayed out from his frozen glare.

'You thought I was eager to wed *you*?' His accent thickened, the only sign of emotion as he stood ramrod-straight. 'You think I delighted in the prospect of marrying a Mangano? That I wanted a bride of that tainted blood? A spoiled, irresponsible trouble-maker who…' He reined in the thread of vitriolic accusation, his mouth flattening in a hard line of contempt.

'You know why I countenanced the match. It had nothing to do with desire for such a wife as you.'

That put her in her place! Alissa felt at a complete disadvantage, bedraggled and shivery, bruised by the sheer force of his personality. She dragged in a breath and slid clammy palms down her damp skirt, searching for a poise she was far from feeling.

'No, you wanted the Sicilian estate I'd bring as dowry. A crumbling castle and overgrown vineyards.' It was unbelievable that he set such store in stones, mortar and soil. Enough to agree to an arranged marriage to a woman he'd never met. Enough to collaborate with Gianfranco Mangano, the man he abhorred.

Dario Parisi was a tycoon with more wealth than he could spend in a lifetime, and still he wanted more. Her grandfather had been the same. They'd vied for the same property, using it and her to further their bitter feud.

His nostrils pinched and his jaw tightened till his neck corded with tension. Those were the only indicators of his struggle to restrain his fury. His face remained impassive, his gaze unreadable.

He obviously had a right royal temper, yet he knew how to control it. If it had been the old man, he'd have lashed out by now, incensed at her for standing up to him.

'I can't believe you bought Jason off.' She paced away from him, needing distance from his imposing presence. 'It must have cost you.'

'Your boyfriend is easily tempted.' Dario's gaze didn't leave her face, yet she had the uncomfortable feeling his attention trawled over her. Heat rose in her throat and she turned to pace again, avoiding that skewering stare.

'Obviously Mr Donnelly didn't feel your…charms were enough to entice him to go through with the deal.'

Her charms! Didn't he realise Jason was gay? But then Jason didn't wear his sexuality on his sleeve.

'You came all the way from Sicily just to stop my marriage?' She paused to shaft a glance at him. 'You must hate the Manganos very much.' The shudder ricocheting through her had nothing to do with her wet clothes.

He shrugged, and this time the movement was anything but insouciant. 'Your family stole from mine. Cheated mine. Deprived me of my birthright, thieving not only my family's home but also the opportunities that should have been mine. Did you ever think of that as you enjoyed your comfortable life? Did you spare a thought for those whose misfortunes laid the foundations for your luxurious lifestyle?'

Fury radiated from his glittering eyes, the steel-grey of a

drawn sword. His posture was aggressive, like that of a man poised to destroy.

Alissa opened her mouth to tell him her life hadn't been one of luxury, but of punishment and fear. Yet he wouldn't believe her. He'd seen her grandfather's home, the grandest in that district of Victoria. He'd believe what he wanted to believe.

Just as the local townspeople had found it convenient to believe Gianfranco was a devoted old man who lavished care and luxury on his granddaughters. Far easier than facing the truth, that the pillar of society was a miserly sadist who spent a small fortune entertaining dignitaries to build his prestige but who thought nothing of sentencing his granddaughters to a week of bread and water for the slightest disobedience.

'Well? Nothing to say?'

She looked up into heavily lidded eyes, ignoring the flutter of tension in her stomach as she met his scathing glare. It wasn't her fault Dario Parisi was caught up in the destructive vendetta between their families.

'I'm not responsible for my grandfather's actions.'

'So you admit he did wrong?'

Alissa's lips firmed at the recollection of Gianfranco's crimes. The memories were so vivid she found her hands clasped together, white-knuckled and shaking.

Carefully she unknotted her fingers and let her hands fall. The past was the past. It was that knowledge which had enabled her to turn her life around, hers and Donna's.

'He did many things that were wrong. Perhaps now he's paying for them.' He'd been frightened enough by the looming prospect of death to leave his estate to the church, trying to atone for a lifetime of sins. All except the Sicilian property. He'd used that to try manipulating her one last time.

'Don't expect me to shoulder his guilt.' She stared back boldly, refusing to be intimidated. After what she'd survived a tongue-lashing was nothing. More important was the vital question of how to meet the terms of the will and get the inheritance she so desperately needed.

'Can I help you?' A disapproving voice made Alissa spin round. A woman in a navy suit glared at them from an open doorway. Alissa opened her mouth to apologise for intruding but Dario forestalled her.

'*Chiedo scusa.* We shouldn't be here, I know.' He lifted his shoulders and spread his open hands and smiled.

Even from where Alissa stood to one side, that smile was spectacular. It transformed his face from censorious and autocratic to warm, attractive and, she hated to admit it, downright *sexy*.

She blinked but the metamorphosis remained in place. He looked a completely different man. If she hadn't known what sort of guy Dario Parisi was she'd have thought him stunning. Even his eyes sparkled with charming, rueful apology. And that smile…

He was more dangerous than she'd thought!

The sheer force of his personality and his absolute determination to get what he wanted made him formidable enough. But with a charm that made even Alissa's pulse quicken? Definitely a man to beware.

The office worker didn't think so. Her frown melted and a smile hovered on her prim mouth as she heard his glib explanation, liberally peppered with Italian phrases. Cynically Alissa wondered if they were a deliberate part of the charming-Mediterranean-male persona he'd adopted.

It was only when he used the words 'my fiancée' and stepped close that she focused on the content of his spiel. She jerked out of reach as he explained how he and his fiancée needed privacy to discuss a personal matter.

Alissa glared, but her anger only corroborated the implication they'd had a lovers' tiff. Before she could set the record straight the other woman was actually apologising that she couldn't let them use her office as she had urgent work to do.

Unbelievable!

'No, no, you mustn't apologise. We have intruded here long enough.' He turned to Alissa. 'Come, *cara*.'

Alissa nodded at the now beaming woman and walked stiff-legged from the room, speeding up when she felt the proprietorial warmth of his touch in the small of her back.

She didn't pause as they walked outside. The rain had eased and she marched down the steps, too aware of Dario beside her. He was infuriating, impossible and an undoubted threat. Yet she couldn't ignore a tiny thrill of awareness at his long, lean body so close to hers.

She must be going crazy.

'In here, *fidanzatina mia*.'

'I'm not your little fiancée.' The words shot out of her mouth, indignation flaring anew. Her Italian was rusty but that she understood. 'We don't have an audience now so you can drop the act.'

She turned to see him inviting her to enter a limo, complete with tinted windows and a chauffeur standing to attention at the door. It was in a 'No Stopping' zone and the chauffeur, despite his suit, looked more like a burly bodyguard than a mere driver. More reminders of Dario's status and wealth.

'I'm not going anywhere in that.' Not with Dario Parisi. Especially not in a limo with blacked-out windows, driven by a goon.

'We have things to discuss.' The thread of almost-temper wove through his words, though his face gave nothing away. 'You know it. This isn't finished.'

Unfortunately he was right. Alissa would have loved to stalk away and never see him again. But that wasn't going to happen. Her shoulders slumped as weariness and worry took their toll. What choice did she have?

'OK.' She paused, thinking rapidly. 'There's a decent café two blocks away. We should find a quiet table.'

Silently he regarded her as if she were some unique specimen.

Perhaps she was, refusing to kowtow to him. She'd bet a lot of women would just say 'Yes, Dario. Whatever you say, Dario', blinded by his wealth and fatal charm.

Even now the memory of his sexy smile warmed a shocked part of her.

'*Daccordo*. Come on, then. Lead the way.' He gestured her forward and paused to speak to the chauffeur.

You will be marrying me instead. His words resounded in her head as she walked. The words she'd steadfastly refused to think about for the last few minutes.

Could it be true? Could that be why he'd come to Australia? To claim her as his bride?

The idea sent a chill of trepidation through her. She tugged her shoulder bag on more securely and hugged her arms tight across her torso.

Dario Parisi's bride...the very fate she'd been so determined to avoid.

How she'd paid for her determination that last year in the old man's house. He'd never forgiven her refusal to comply with his scheme to link the two families.

She should have left home then, but she'd felt compelled to stay till Donna was legally old enough to leave home too. Donna had been her responsibility for as long as she could remember. She'd never leave her little sister alone to their grandfather's tender mercies.

Absently she rubbed at her wrist, remembering Gianfranco's reaction when she'd rejected the marriage he'd schemed to bring about.

'You're getting wet.' The deep voice curled like smoke through her memories, drawing her back to the present.

She turned her head to find Dario walking beside her, holding an enormous umbrella over them both. Heat from his body transferred the few centimetres to hers: her arm, her shoulder, her hip and thigh. And further, spreading through her shock-numbed body. Latent energy sizzled off him in waves, sparking tingles of awareness.

What was this man? Some sort of power generator?

Her pulse quickened and so did her pace. She didn't like the illusion of intimacy as he sheltered her from the rain. The world beyond the umbrella was an anonymous blur, cocooning them together as the soft rain became a downpour.

It didn't seem to bother him, though the rain angled down so his legs must be getting wet. Had he chosen her left side to shelter her from a soaking? Surely not. This man was no protector.

'Thank you,' she murmured eventually, forcing the words through her tense lips, 'for the umbrella.'

He looked at her then. She could no longer see the gleam of anger in his eyes or stark impatience. But his expression made her stomach muscles spasm tight, her breath falter. She read speculation and something that looked almost like possessiveness.

No! Abruptly she looked away. There was no expression in his eyes. Nothing at all.

'Here. This is it.' Alissa didn't care if she sounded desperate to see the café. She plunged under its awning and pushed open the door, not waiting for him.

Dario shook the umbrella and followed her inside. She scurried in, spoke briefly to the waiter and took a seat with her back to the wall. The choice indicated Alissa Scott felt under threat. She had that much sense then.

Her jerky movements as she patted at her hair and fussed over her bag gave her away too. As did her furtive glances in his direction.

He dropped the umbrella inside the door, nodded at the waiter and strolled across the room, enjoying the way Alissa's eyes widened at his approach.

Obviously she hadn't bothered to discover what he looked like before today and his appearance was a surprise. The implied dismissal smarted. Yet though she tried to hide it, part of her response to him was feminine interest. Dario had been on the receiving end of female stares since adolescence. He could read those hot, guilty glances in a second.

One more piece of knowledge to use to his advantage. Who knew? Dealing with the recalcitrant Ms Scott might have unexpected bonuses.

He dragged out a chair and took a seat. His long legs tangled with hers till she shifted away.

What was he thinking? She was a cute little package, if one liked that sort of thing. But he was more discerning. Cheap goods weren't to his taste.

The waiter was there as he settled in his seat.

'Espresso,' Dario murmured, not shifting his gaze from Alissa's wide blue gaze. 'And...?'

'Hot chocolate.'

At his raised brows she muttered, 'I don't need a stimulant in my bloodstream.'

Why? Because she'd already taken something to see her through the day? No, she was sober enough. No sign of drug use. He'd scrutinised her carefully.

'I just want to get warm.'

Despite the streaks of hectic colour on her cheeks she was pale. Stress? Shock? Annoyance at having her avaricious scheme ruined? He felt no sympathy at all.

Leaning back, he stretched his legs and shoved his hands in his pockets. She'd go nowhere till he was ready.

The silence grew thick. Dario was in no haste to break it. He knew how to use it to unnerve an adversary. What was the point in rushing? The outcome was a foregone conclusion. Let her sweat a little longer.

Yet she didn't fidget. Her spine was straight and her gaze steady. Her attitude piqued his interest. She wasn't easily intimidated. That surprised him. He'd expected her to have little stamina and no grit.

The waiter left their drinks and Dario watched Alissa cradle her mug. She closed her eyes and inhaled on a sigh of pleasure that spiked heat straight through his belly.

Porca miseria! That wasn't supposed to happen. Not with her. Just because he could imagine that Cupid's-bow mouth pouting under his, sighing out a very different kind of pleasure as those slim, neat hands caressed his...

'Are you going to tell me now, or are you enjoying trying to intimidate me?' she asked in a low voice.

Those remarkable eyes, the colour of the sea on a clear day, fixed on his. Her mouth twisted in a tiny wry smile that belied her defensive posture. She was a fighter.

'You know why I'm here.'

She lowered the mug, but kept her fingers wrapped round it as if needing its warmth.

'The Sicilian estate.'

'The Castello Parisi.' He nodded, using its proper name and feeling the inevitable surge of pride.

'You want it.' Her voice was flat, giving nothing away. Her gaze dropped to her hot chocolate.

'Can you doubt it?'

She shook her head once. 'No. You badgered the old man for it long enough.'

'Badgered!' He leaned forward till she raised her face. Her eyes were enormous, but if she expected sympathy she had the wrong man. 'To offer *more* than a fair price for what is rightfully mine? For what the unscrupulous old devil stole from my family? The home of my family for generations?'

The heat in his belly now had nothing to do with sexual awareness and everything to do with outraged pride and the desire for justice.

Until the *castello* was in his hands, once again the jewel in the crown of the now vast Parisi holdings, all his success was hollow. It was his home, his past, the family he no longer had.

His identity, proof that he was worthy of his proud name. Dario had promised his father the day he died that he'd recover it. Nothing would make him break that oath.

'I know the story,' she said slowly. 'Gianfranco bought it when your family fell on hard times, promising to sell it back when they recouped their losses.'

'He bought it for a fraction of its worth.' Hatred for the man who'd destroyed the Parisis sent adrenalin surging through his blood. 'Did he also tell you it was his underhand dealings, his dishonesty that ruined us in the first place? That he'd set out to destroy the family he'd once called friends?'

He didn't wait for an answer. 'Do you have any idea how it stuck in my craw to negotiate with that man? The niceties of business were too good for him. In an earlier time I would just have taken it from him.'

'By force?' Alissa looked into those metal-grey eyes and wondered how she'd ever imagined warmth there. His gaze was glacier-cold, frozen with a hate that made her shiver.

She shuddered and pushed her chair back from the table as dread curdled her stomach.

'I'm a law-abiding man,' Dario Parisi drawled, but his expression told her how he would have enjoyed inflicting a very personal vengeance on her grandfather.

Two of a kind. That's what they were. Just as she'd always suspected.

That was why Gianfranco had been so determined Alissa marry this hard-faced stranger. Partly for the satisfaction of seeing a Parisi marry his granddaughter. The feud had begun when a Parisi jilted Gianfranco's sister and he'd carried a chip on his shoulder ever since. But mainly because 'He'll put up with none of your nonsense, girl. He'll knock you into shape and keep you under control. A good, old-fashioned Sicilian husband with a hard hand'.

Her breath came in shallow gulps as she fought for calm. She was safe. Dario Parisi couldn't harm her.

'What's that?' She found her voice as he took a document from his suit pocket and spread it on the table.

'You need to complete it so it can be lodged today.' He reached back into his pocket and drew out a gold fountain pen, placing it neatly on the table beside the official-looking document.

Foreboding slammed into her. She couldn't sell him the estate; he knew that. So what was he asking her to sign?

Reluctantly she leaned forward and read the title.

Notice of Intention to Marry.

The breath whooshed from her lungs like air from a pierced balloon. She'd signed one when she and Jason had planned to wed. But this time the names were different.

Alissa Serena Scott and Dario Pasquale Tommaso Parisi.

CHAPTER THREE

'YOU can't be serious!' Alissa stared, heart sinking. Yet instinctively she knew Dario was absolutely serious about marrying her. Correction: marrying the Parisi estate.

She slumped, her energy draining away. She'd come full circle. After years fighting the old man's manipulative schemes, had she no choice now but to do as he'd always planned? Marry Dario Parisi and force his aristocratic family to accept a Mangano into the fold? Take as her husband a man every bit as dangerous as the old tartar who'd made her life hell?

'Your display of feminine vulnerability is charming,' murmured a deep, gravelly voice, 'but it's wasted. You could have made this easy. Instead you chose the hard way.'

Her head shot up. 'You blame *me* for this mess?'

'If the cap fits…' He looked so at ease, sipping his espresso, his dark suit parted casually, like a model in a glossy lifestyle magazine. Except no paid model would ever wear that lethally calculating expression.

'We could have married several years ago when I first agreed to the idea.'

Her grandfather's idea. Dario had only agreed after Gianfranco rejected offer after offer to buy the Sicilian estate. He'd vowed the only way a Parisi would get his hands on it was to marry her.

Alissa had refused. And she'd paid for her disobedience.

Absently she ran a finger over her wrist, a nervous gesture tha stopped under Dario's scrutiny.

'I suppose your need for funds wasn't so urgent then. You grandfather was alive to indulge you.'

Alissa almost laughed aloud at the idea of being indulged by the old man. 'Or perhaps I just objected to marrying you.' She put her palms on the table. She'd had enough of his jibes and hi self-assurance. She wished she could find some vulnerability i him. But his only response was a quirk of the lips as if her ripost amused him.

'That doesn't bother you?' She lifted her chin.

'Our marriage isn't a meeting of minds. Or a consummatio of romantic love. It's business. Otherwise I would not contem plate marrying a woman like you.'

He spoke through a chilling half-smile and Alissa shivered *Ruthless.* That was Dario Parisi. She felt a net draw inextricabl tighter around her, leaving no way out.

She'd thought she knew all about ruthless men. But the wa his relaxed demeanour cloaked bone-deep obsession gave a whol new perspective on the type. Foreboding sliced through her. H was relentless, biding his time patiently for years as he waited t acquire the property he wanted. And acquire *her* in the process

He leaned close, the smile sliding off his face. 'You shoul have accepted the offer I made after your grandfather died Marriage, a quick divorce and a handsome settlement in retur for your share of the estate.'

Except she'd wanted nothing to do with her grandfather' property. She'd had no qualms giving up her chance for wealth especially with such strings attached. When her lawyer told he of Dario's second proposal after her grandfather's death, she' rejected it instantly.

'I didn't want the estate then,' she murmured.

'No, you thought you could challenge the will and inheri

alone, without the inconvenience of sharing with me.' Suspicion darkened his gaze. 'Greed runs strong in your family.'

'You should talk!' She leaned towards him, recklessly disregarding the zap of electricity that sheared between them as their glares clashed. 'You'll do anything to get your hands on the *castello*.'

This close she saw the fine-grained texture of his skin, the shadow darkening his chin. She inhaled the scent of spicy male skin and citrus and her nostrils quivered.

Too close screamed a warning voice in her head as each sense came alive to his presence. Alarm bells jangled as her heartbeat revved and her skin prickled.

Before she could move large hands captured hers, imprisoning them on the table. Long fingers linked around her wrists. Heat radiated from his touch.

'No doubt you also inherited a hatred of my family. You were determined to keep for yourself what's mine.'

She shook her head. 'No. I just didn't want the money.' Not until the news that Donna needed help.

The impact of his unblinking regard and his handsome, brooding face was devastating. She jerked her hands, trying to break free.

His encircling fingers didn't loosen. To an onlooker they'd seem like lovers. He was so intense, his wide shoulders crowding her in, cutting her off from the room.

'Don't lie. You grew up with money and you're feeling the pinch now you have to fend for yourself.' He paused. 'It must have been a shock to find Gianfranco had left most of his estate to charity.' One sleek, dark brow rose speculatively. 'You fell out with him.'

'You could say that.'

He shook his head. 'I know about your…habits. They don't come cheap.' His face hardened, grooves appearing beside his mouth. 'Even though you seem to have cleaned up your act lately, your record with designer drugs shows you have expensive tastes.'

Alissa goggled. He knew about *that*? Nausea churned in her stomach at the memories he'd dredged up. Bile choked her. This man knew about her past and judged her with such matter-of-fact contempt. Yet still he wanted to marry her!

How badly he wanted that land.

Looking into his wintry, judgemental eyes, she wanted to blurt out that she'd never taken drugs in her life. That she'd been innocent.

She couldn't. Only one other person knew the truth. The person she'd vowed to protect, even at the cost of her reputation. She'd gladly shouldered the blame and accepted the consequences. It was too late to change the record now. Besides, Dario Parisi was so biased he'd never believe her.

'You had me investigated,' she said flatly.

'Of course.' He slid a thumb along the side of her hand in a mockery of a caress. To her horror her skin drew tight and shivery. 'Even to gain my birthright, I would not walk into marriage without knowing my bride.'

He lingered over the last word with a deliberation that set her teeth on edge. She felt trapped. Claustrophobia gnawed the edges of her consciousness. She fought it, refusing to let it drag her under. She tried to slip one hand free, but his hold was implacable.

'Why wait till today to buy Jason off?' She hurried into speech, unnerved by his waiting silence.

'My staff contacted Mr Donnelly as soon as you sought permission to marry.'

'You organised this weeks ago?' Her eyes widened as she took in his satisfied expression.

'As if I'd leave it to chance! While you expected to marry him I knew exactly what your plans were.'

'And by having him jilt me today, you cut off my options.' The air was expelled from her lungs. 'I have to marry within a month to inherit.' She breathed deep, ignoring the acid taste of fear on her tongue. 'And in Australia we have to give a month's notice before marriage. Which means—'

'You just ran out of alternatives.' His smile didn't reach his eyes. 'Unless you have another bridegroom tucked up your sleeve?' He paused and stroked an insolent finger along her wrist. Her pulse jumped and she gritted her teeth, furious with him and with her traitorous body that didn't know the enemy when he sat before her.

'No one else willing to sign a document like this—' he nodded at the paper beneath her hands '—before close of business today?'

His sarcasm made her blood boil. 'You manipulative, arrogant, cocksure—'

'Now, now, Alissa. Is that any way to talk to the one man who can give you what you want?' His gaze roved over her with a provocative thoroughness that was the final straw.

'Take your hands off me. Now!' She didn't raise her voice but raw fury throbbed in each word.

His brows arched. His fingers loosened. She slid her hands into her lap and cradled them, trying to ignore the heat of his touch lingering on her skin. Trying to conquer her fear.

She wanted to shove her chair back and walk out, alone. Never see Dario Parisi's gorgeous fallen-angel face or hear his mocking, sexy voice again.

The trouble was she lived in the real world, with responsibilities she couldn't shirk. People she cared for. Cold iced her bones and she reached for her mug, seeking its residual warmth.

'By the terms of the will I have to live with my husband for six months before we jointly inherit.'

He nodded. 'We'll divorce as soon as the land is ours. Then you sell your share of the property to me, for the current market price, of course.' He sounded as if he discussed a routine financial transaction. Not marriage.

Alissa's heart beat fast at the idea of living with Dario Parisi. Could she survive six months with this man who looked at her with such condemnation, but whose touch turned her inside out?

'But it means *living together*.'

He watched her speculatively. 'That bothers you? Living with me?' If she weren't so keyed up Alissa would be insulted by his surprise. As if trusting herself to the care of a stranger was no big deal. What did he think she was? A tart as well as a drug addict?

'I knew Jason. I could trust him.' That seemed stupid since he'd duped her, but she'd known they'd be platonic flatmates and no more.

'Ah.' The syllable stretched out, like her nerves. 'You want assurance your abundant charms won't incite me to seduce you.' His gaze dipped to her jacket buttons and searing heat coiled in her stomach.

Alissa kept her mouth firmly shut against the protest that she'd never let a man like him seduce her.

'You have my word as a Parisi. I would never force a woman. Besides—' his lips curved in a half-smile that held no humour '—your type is not to my taste.'

Her type. Her *type*!

'I understand completely.' Alissa pasted on a saccharine smile, despite the protest of muscles taut with horror. 'I can't think of a man less appealing than you.'

It was minuscule compensation to see him taken aback by her statement. But, boy, it felt good.

Just as well he couldn't know she lied. Dario Parisi didn't appeal. But maybe with a personality transplant...that strong, lean body, the mobile, sensuous mouth and well-shaped hands...he was the sexiest man she'd ever seen. Fate didn't play fair.

'Excellent,' Dario murmured, thrusting aside annoyance at her insult. 'Then there will be no complications.'

He'd get what he wanted and dump Alissa Scott like lightning. Tying himself to a woman tainted not just by her Mangano blood but also by self-indulgence, avarice and low personal standards appalled him.

After the *castello* was safe he'd find the perfect wife. *That*

Signora Parisi would be elegant, refined, sweet-tempered. Not a sharp-tongued virago who challenged with every stare, sidetracked his thoughts and stirred his hormones at inconvenient times.

They'd raise a houseful of *bambini*. He'd possess everything he'd dreamt of in the days when he had nothing but pride and determination. He remembered how it felt to be hungry and alone. *Never again.*

He'd have it all. Respect, wealth, power, the birthright he'd been denied. And a family of his own, flesh of his flesh.

Yet Alissa's jibe rankled. His looks and vast wealth made him irresistible to most women. She was no different. He'd seen the flare of awareness in her wide blue eyes.

Despite his strict code of honour that tempered the drive to succeed, he'd been accused of many things as he forged his way to the top of the corporate heap. Usually by unsuccessful competitors or journalists whose stock-in-trade was exaggeration. Why did her insult needle him like a splinter embedded deep?

'We know where we stand. *Si?* There will be no misunderstandings.'

The last thing he wanted was for her to try her feminine wiles on him. He had no patience with importunate women, even if they radiated sexual allure like this one. There was dynamite in the sway of her hips, her lush mouth and in the feminine curves her cheap suit couldn't hide.

Yet her huge, shadowed eyes looked vulnerable.

Nonsense. She was a calculating little piece. She'd deliberately stymied his chances to regain the estate, once when her grandfather proposed a merger and again after his death. She'd gone to great lengths to thwart Dario and keep the estate to herself and her weak-chinned boyfriend.

He had to remember Alissa Scott was his enemy.

No misunderstandings. Could she trust his word?

He despised her, so he couldn't want her. Could he? What

about the sizzle of masculine speculation in his eyes? To her relatively inexperienced eye that looked like the stare of a man who was all too interested.

Was it possible his archaic ideas about family vendettas meant he wanted retribution? The *personal* satisfaction of seducing a woman he saw as his enemy?

No! Her imagination was out of control.

Alissa squeezed her eyes shut, wishing she could open them to discover this was a dream.

'Alissa?'

No one else said her name like that. A rumbling purr that made it sound interesting…seductive. That made her nape prickle and her breasts tighten.

Reluctantly she opened her eyes. Dario Parisi watched her with the attention a scientist gave a newly discovered species, missing nothing.

'A business arrangement.' She forced the words out.

He nodded.

'I suppose you've thought about where we'd live?'

'Naturally you'll come to Sicily. My home is there.'

'Naturally.' She doubted he noticed her sarcasm. It wouldn't occur to him that she had reasons to stay in Australia. A job, a home, a sister she loved and feared for. 'I'd have to give up my job.'

Grey eyes held hers. 'In six months you'll have enough money not to need a job.'

What would he say if she told him she loved her work? Enjoyed helping people plan their holidays? Had a flair for dealing with even the most hard-to-please clients?

It didn't matter. Nothing mattered except saving Donna. Even if it meant spending six months under the same roof as a condescending, manipulative Sicilian male.

Been there. Done that. Survived.

She looked at the paper between them. The details had been completed, even hers. He was frighteningly thorough.

Could she really be planning to agree? Shock held her rigid as she absorbed the enormity of what she risked. She was caught fast, she had no choice. But surely Dario was vulnerable too. His obsession with regaining the estate must give her leverage in this unholy bargain.

'If I agree—' she met his stare without blinking '—I want an advance. A third of the *castello*'s value on the day we marry.' Her heart thundered. The money meant nothing to him. He had plenty. To her it meant immediate treatment for Donna. The specialists said she had time, could wait, but this way there'd be no delay.

'Well?' Alissa lifted her chin, her palms growing damp. 'Your bankers could arrange it easily.'

'No doubt they could.' He left the sentence hang till her nerves shredded to tatters. 'You've inherited your grandfather's instinct for screwing cash out of people.' The deadly chill in his tone thrust her back in her chair.

His glare now was pure threat. Pure hatred. Each clipped word a shard of ice on her unprotected skin.

'Very clever, Alissa. You know I want the *castello*. I'll even marry *you* to get it.' His emphasis on the word made her feel like something that had scuttled from under a rock. 'But there I draw the line. I won't be manipulated any further by your family. Every man has his limit and I've reached mine. You Manganos have pushed me as far as I'm willing to go.' He leaned across and held her captive with a coruscating look.

'If you want any more you can whistle for it. I might be constrained by the terms of the will, but so are you, *fidanzatina mia*.' His lips curled in a smile that chilled her blood. 'This is the *only* deal on the table. If you want more, find some other man.'

Alissa shuddered. A lifetime's memories of fear and vulnerability flooded back as she met his merciless gaze. He had the upper hand because he was powerful and rich. Even if he had to wait for years and expend a fortune, he'd find a way to get the estate in the end.

She had no other options.

'It's an hour before the registry closes.' He glanced at his discreet gold watch. 'Then you miss the deadline.'

Alissa smoothed trembling hands over her skirt. She straightened her spine and reached for the pen, ignoring the voice inside that shrieked dire warnings.

This felt wrong. But it was the only way to make things right. 'Where do I sign?'

Dario paced the foyer, resisting the urge to check the time. She was on her way; he'd just had an update on her movements.

He strode to the entrance, fists deep in his pockets. He'd never been so keyed up before a deal. Regaining his family home meant more than buying or selling companies. This wasn't about mere cash, but about family, his very identity. This quest had been his sole purpose for as long as he could remember.

It went against the grain marrying a woman shallow enough to sell herself to acquire a fortune she could fritter away. But no sacrifice was too great.

His gaze fixed on a passing teenager, all fly-away hair and bare legs. Instantly the memory he'd repressed so often filled his mind. Alissa the first time he'd seen her. A few years ago, when he'd grown impatient of long-distance negotiations and visited Gianfranco Mangano. The old weasel had insisted only marriage would secure the Parisi estate.

Dario had sat in his car after the fruitless meeting, trying to find the bait to make Mangano sell. That was when he'd seen her, sneaking into the house in the dark.

He recalled the sultry length of her legs as she climbed out of the low car in her miniskirt. The throaty laugh of a woman sharing a joke with her lover. Her long hair flicked provocatively over one shoulder, a glimpse of pert breasts and a profile that stopped his breath.

His body had responded with a primal throb of hunger neither pride nor logic could prevent. The old man had let slip a thing or two about his granddaughter and her wild ways. He'd wanted her safely married and off his hands.

From that one glimpse Dario knew she wasn't the sort to have marriage on her mind. A judgement confirmed when he heard of her later drug conviction.

Yet he'd never been able to rid himself of that image of carefree, sensual beauty. Even now something about Alissa Scott made his hormones stand up and salivate. It was a reaction he wasn't proud of.

A blur of movement caught his eye and he turned.

Porca miseria! She couldn't be serious.

His lips thinned as she approached, his temper rising to boiling point. Had she no self-respect? She made a mockery of them both.

His gaze swept over his wife-to-be, climbing the steps towards him. Heads turned to watch. She wore satin and lace, a long white dress with a froth of skirts and a dragging train. A fussy veil obscured her face, no doubt hiding a triumphant smirk at his expense.

'I don't remember specifying fancy dress.' His provocative drawl slid across her flesh like ice. Alissa clenched her jaw and continued up the stairs, ignoring him.

She felt sick to her stomach about the wedding. The last thing she needed was sarcasm.

For two pins she'd…what? Run away?

She didn't have that luxury. The knowledge weighed her down, like shackles on a condemned prisoner. She drew a sustaining breath then wished she hadn't as the bodice, a size too small, constricted her lungs.

'Hello, Dario. As charming as ever, I see.'

He was too big, too daunting, too…unsettling. Tension squirmed in her stomach and her pulse tripped as she caught the scent of lemon and warm male flesh.

Her body conspired against her, responding to his overt masculinity with an excitement that appalled her. She lifted her skirts and hurried up the last of the stairs.

'What's the meaning of this?' He stepped in front of her so she had no alternative but to meet his steely gaze. Glacial ice couldn't be colder than the look he gave her.

'This?' She tilted her chin.

'The masquerade costume.' He spoke through barely parted lips and she had the satisfaction of knowing that no matter how terrible she felt wearing Donna's precious bridal dress, her bridegroom hated it more. Good. Let that be some small compensation for the distress he'd caused.

'Haven't you seen a bride before?' she taunted.

'But you're not a bride in the usual sense.'

For that she was thankful. The idea of a real marriage, of intimacy with Dario, was too devastating.

'What do you care?' She moved sideways but he blocked her, filling her vision, dominating her senses.

'Why do you insist on this charade?' he snarled.

Alissa slipped a hand under the veil and rubbed her temple where a tension headache throbbed.

'As I'm moving to Italy I had to explain to people I was getting married. There was no need when I'd planned to stay in Melbourne.' He said nothing, just stood, waiting. 'My sister is sentimental. She married recently. She believes in romantic love with all the trimmings.'

'So you lied about this marriage? To your sister?' There was condemnation in the deep timbre of his voice.

Alissa shrugged. 'It was easier to let her believe I'd been swept off my feet. When we divorce it will seem a case of marry in haste and repent at leisure.' She wouldn't add to Donna's worries by revealing the true reason for the wedding. She'd be racked with guilt, knowing Alissa had married for her sake, and Dario Parisi of all men.

'That doesn't explain the costume.'

'Donna wanted to be here but I persuaded her not to.' Even her loving sister had seen it made more sense to save to see a specialist in the USA than cross the country for a wedding. 'She asked me to wear her dress. You know, something borrowed…' Her words petered out under his critical stare. 'I promised her I'd wear it. OK?'

'And you keep your promises?'

Did he have to sound so sceptical? It was a good thing she didn't care about his opinion. This was just a business deal. A charade to satisfy the terms of a will.

Yet, wearing her borrowed finery, dwarfed by his ultra-masculine presence, Alissa felt a thread of something unexpected weave through her. A tremor of awareness. Dario was still the sexiest man she'd laid eyes on.

Pity he was an arrogant jerk.

'If you've finished finding fault, can we go in? We don't want to miss our appointment.'

Silently he took her arm and escorted her inside, a parody of the solicitous lover.

After that everything was a blur. Nothing seemed real, not the weight of the dress, or the way her hand fitted snugly in his. When he produced a ring, a glittering proclamation of wealth and status, she wasn't even surprised that it fitted perfectly.

Only as the celebrant said, 'You may now kiss the bride,' did the comfortable illusion of unreality splinter.

Dario turned her round, his hands heavily proprietorial at her waist, and heat radiated through her. She read triumph in his eyes. Satisfaction.

That was when it hit her full force. She'd just married a man who could make her life hell.

Panic clawed at Alissa. She fought for oxygen, her breathing hampered by the too-tight bodice. Blood rushed so loud in her ears she heard nothing else.

Deft hands drew the veil up. Without its protection his scrutiny was razor sharp, his smile knowing. It was the satisfied look of a rapacious marauder, not a dispassionate businessman. And it confirmed what she'd feared.

This was personal.

Before she could protest his lips covered her mouth.

Instinctively she lifted her hands and pushed with all her might against the hard-muscled wall of his chest. It was warm, weighty, alive with the throb of his heart and as immovable as the building in which they stood.

His hands at her waist were deceptively loose. When she backed away they tightened possessively, holding her still. No mistaking that encircling grip for anything more tender than an imprisoning grasp.

His mouth touched hers. More than touched, it caressed, blazing a trail of molten heat across her lips. His kiss was slow, deliberate and provocative. Masterful. His lips were soft but insistent. Surprisingly seductive. He tasted of rich, honeyed darkness, of mystery. The musky male scent of heat and spice clouded her bemused brain.

Alissa's eyes widened as she registered pleasure at his skilful caress. A tiny spark of feminine appreciation. A rippling tide of awareness that heated her blood.

Ruthlessly she crushed it, ignoring too the sizzle of unexpected pleasure as his hands all but spanned her waist, making her feel dainty, feminine and delicate.

Desperately she focused on pushing him away. Yet her efforts had no effect. He swamped her senses till she was aware of nothing but his hot, heady presence and the current of desire threatening to drag her under. A slow-turning twist of unfamiliar tension coiled deep inside her.

Eventually he lifted his head and she stared, dumbfounded, at the man who was her husband. She hadn't expected him to kiss her. More, she couldn't believe his kiss had been so…disturbing. How could she have responded to a man she didn't want?

Dark grey eyes surveyed her as thoroughly as she scrutinised him. His gaze was unrevealing but for a shadow of expression that flickered for an instant.

A firm hand grasped her sagging jaw. 'Time enough to stare later, *moglie mia.*' His whisper was sardonic.

Moglie mia. My wife. Alissa's heart plunged in free fall as she absorbed the horrifying finality of those words. There was no going back.

He steered her to a desk so she could sign the marriage certificate. Absurdly she was grateful for his support. Her legs felt like cotton wool, her mind was muzzy with shock.

Why had he kissed her?

Because he can. It's a power thing.

Yet, watching his tight-lipped profile as he signed his name in a slashing script, Alissa could no longer read satisfaction on his face. He looked grimmer than ever.

Perhaps he didn't like kissing her. She tried to take comfort in the thought. But her brain was stuck in shocked awareness of how devastating his kiss had been.

It must never happen again.

Dario watched the witnesses sign the vital paper that finally secured his ownership of the family estate.

That bound him to Alissa Scott. Alissa Parisi now.

His wife. Distaste filled him. She sat motionless, bedecked in showy white satin and a froth of gauzy veil. Who did she think she fooled with that virginal outfit? She was no innocent.

Was the gown an obscure joke or had she been serious about dressing to please her sister? The notion didn't sit well with what he knew of this woman.

Grasping, immoral, unrepentant. She'd tried so hard to deny

him ownership of his home. She must have imbibed the Mangano hatred of Parisi blood with her mother's milk.

Yet he'd made her his wife.

The Parisi name shouldn't be sullied in such a way.

He ignored the turbulent heat that fired his bloodstream whenever their gazes met. The way his eyes strayed to her face. Her neat nose, bluer-than-blue eyes, her perfect mouth, the fragility of her slender neck.

He was merely taking her measure. It was anger he felt, not desire. He remembered the feel of her flagrantly enticing body, his hands encircling her tiny waist. The taste of her, rich and sweet. The tattoo of need that throbbed in his blood as he inhaled her skin's perfume. The pulse of need he couldn't suppress.

Triumph had tempted him to respond to the lure of her petal-soft lips. They'd fascinated him from the first. Now he knew they were lush, delicious, dangerously enticing.

The kiss had been an error.

It must never happen again.

CHAPTER FOUR

THEY emerged from the building into bright sunlight. Brilliant blue sky mocked Alissa's foreboding.

'Mr Parisi! Dario Parisi!'

Alissa faltered as strident voices called out.

'Hell!' Beside her, Dario gave vent to a stream of vitriolic Italian under his breath. Bewildered, Alissa saw a mob of photographers crowding close.

Dario turned, his shoulder blocking them from her vision. She read the sizzle of fury in his expression.

'That's why you wore the dress? Playing to the media?' His tone could cut solid ice. 'Enjoy it while you can, Signora Parisi. Your day in the limelight will be short.'

'Mr Parisi!' A shout cut across Alissa's denial. 'Have you got a statement about your secret marriage to an Aussie girl?' Cameras thrust close, their lenses threatening dark voids, the sound of shutter clicks aggressive.

'No comment,' Dario said brusquely, keeping her clamped against him as he shouldered his way down the stairs. His arm looped round her in an embrace like the bite of an unyielding iron chain.

'After you.' His clipped tone matched his tight hold.

Alissa stared at the limousine. At the door held open by a

familiar chauffeur. The same tough-looking character who'd followed her this past month.

'No, thank you. I have my own car.' Her ancient red hatchback was a block away.

'Nevertheless,' he paused on the word, his emphasis on the sibilant vaguely sinister, 'we'll travel together.'

Short of an embarrassing public tussle, she had no choice but to let him sweep her into the limo.

Alissa sat stiffly as he bent to tuck in the train of her dress, apparently oblivious to the clustering Press. She caught again the fresh scent of his skin, so warmly enticing. So unlike the rigid precision of the man himself. His black hair was combed severely, not a lock out of place. His collar whiter than white, the cut of his suit perfection, his visage as grimly beautiful as a stone god.

There was nothing soft about him.

As his eyes lifted under level black brows to meet hers, she was stabbed again by the chill of his disapproval. His distaste. And more. Hatred?

Alissa shrank back, heart fluttering. He had what he wanted, the promise of the old *castello*. He couldn't want a more personal form of retribution.

His silence as they sped off did nothing to dispel her unease. Tension built with each wordless kilometre.

'I didn't call the Press,' she finally blurted.

'Spare me your protestations of innocence.' He waved a disparaging hand. 'I have no interest in them.'

'Even if they're the truth?' Indignation sizzled at his presumption of her guilt.

His gaze bored into her, like sharpened steel against her soft flesh. 'I accept you are many things, but don't tax my credulity by pretending innocent is one of them.'

Hot denials trembled on her lips but she bit them back. Instinct told her he was as obstinate as he was self-satisfied. No amount of arguing would persuade him.

Alissa's pulse tripped at the flicker of awareness she read in his hooded eyes. A shimmer of heat flared in the pit of her belly. Despite his formidable control he had the look of a man well-versed in carnal pleasures. That sensuous mouth. Those hands...

Incendiary heat spread under her skin, over her breasts, her throat, to her cheeks.

She couldn't believe she had such thoughts about Dario. It should be easy to hate him for his brutal, domineering tactics, for his overweening pride, for the way he enjoyed her discomfort. Even for the pain he'd unwittingly caused with his first offer of marriage. Alissa had paid a high price for turning him down, enduring the worst ever of her grandfather's beatings.

But, to her horror, it wasn't hatred that stirred as she met his dark gaze. It was something far more primitive. Far more dangerous. Far more...feminine.

If ever Dario guessed, he'd make her life hell.

The setting sun turned the Mediterranean to liquid silk, indigo and pink shot with orange and shafts of gold.

It was beautiful, the exquisite colours, the rugged coastal outcrops, the ancient towns and villages. Yet a chill of trepidation lanced Alissa and she shifted uneasily on the limousine's leather seat.

Sicily. The island that had bred the manipulative, vicious man she'd had to call grandfather. The one place she'd never wanted to visit. The place that had also produced God's gift to himself, Dario Parisi.

Despite the first-class luxury of their flight and the doting attention of staff, Alissa had barely slept. She felt crumpled and stale. Worse, she couldn't shake her anxiety about Donna.

She didn't like leaving while her sister was ill. Yes, Donna was married now, but a lifetime's habit wasn't easily ignored. Alissa had been responsible for her since they were kids. She'd looked out for her, protected her.

She bit her lip, remembering how badly she'd failed her little sister when it really mattered.

Now Donna had David, a man who'd do anything for his bride. They'd be happy together. Donna deserved a chance at happiness after the childhood she'd endured. If only they could get the money for her treatment. Such severe liver damage was beyond the skills of the local medicos. Her only hope of survival lay in a radical new treatment overseas. Expensive treatment. They'd tried everything they could to raise the cash. Unsuccessfully.

Which brought Alissa to Dario Parisi. *Her husband.*

Through the long journey he'd been at ease amidst the extravagant luxury that, though she fought not to show it, unsettled Alissa. A man with that sort of money could get away with almost anything.

He'd slept soundly, as if he didn't have a thing on his conscience. He'd eaten heartily and been brusquely courteous in a way that reinforced his disapproval. Clearly he considered her undeserving of his exalted company!

He was an arrogant, macho dinosaur who considered his word law. His casual acceptance of lavish attention, his impatience at delay bespoke a man of enormous power and ego. Despite his handsome façade he was dangerous. She'd read about his cut-throat business tactics and how he crushed all before him. His reputation with women was no better. His progress was littered with beautiful, disappointed ex-lovers.

Dario sat back, surveying the landscape through narrowed, proprietary eyes as if he owned it all. For all she knew he might! The flight from Rome by luxury private jet was more proof of his stupendous wealth.

'How much further?' They were the first words either had spoken since they'd landed in Sicily.

Alissa could have kicked herself when she saw his mouth twist in a smirk of triumph. Had he hoped she'd snap under his silence?

If that was the worst he could do, he was in for a shock. She'd weathered far worse treatment, meted out by an expert.

When he spoke his voice was like smoky honey. Goose flesh rose across her arms and awareness sizzled. He'd probably spent years perfecting that deep tone. It was guaranteed to get under any woman's skin.

'What?' he purred. 'Aren't you enjoying the view? Most visitors are in raptures over their first sight of Sicily.'

Alissa met his scrutiny for only a moment before turning away. 'Most of them are willing visitors, looking forward to a holiday in the sun.'

'And you're unwilling?' He paused so long she fought the urge to look at him over her hunched shoulder. She was strung out, at the end of her physical and mental reserves. She didn't have the energy for a full-on altercation.

'No one forced you, Alissa. You came of your own free will.' The way he said her name, lingering over the sibilants, drawing out the vowels, made it almost a caress.

He was playing with her, enjoying her discomfort.

'That doesn't deserve an answer.' Dario Parisi and her grandfather had manipulated her into a position where the notion of free will was a joke.

Her husband relished the knowledge. He probably got his kicks out of bullying people who couldn't stand up to him. Or, in her case, besting the woman who'd spurned his offer of marriage not once but twice. No doubt his pride had smarted at the rejection. She'd bet he wasn't used to women denying him what he wanted.

From the corner of her eye she saw a blur of movement. Strong fingers cupped her chin. He didn't use enough force to hurt her, yet she had no option but to turn. His long frame crowded her into the corner of the back seat.

Her heart thumped an uneven tattoo as she inhaled the scent of ripe lemon and fresh man, a warm, earthy tang that made her nostrils flare and her pulse patter.

Heat flushed her body and she leaned back, trying to avoid contact. He shifted his hand, sliding his fingers down her throat, where she was most vulnerable, then round to cup her neck and hold her still. His thumb stroked the sensitive skin below her ear and blood roared, blocking out the hum of the car engine.

'Are you trying to make me feel *sorry* for you?' His dulcet tone was incredulous. 'Do you really think I should have any compunction about how I treat the woman who plotted to deny me my birthright?' He leaned close enough for his breath to feather her mouth.

Despite his leashed anger, there was something almost… erotic about the proximity of his long, mobile mouth with its sensuously full lower lip. She felt each word in puffs of air that ignited explosions of sensation along her own mouth.

It was anger that parched her throat and made her swipe her lips with her tongue. It couldn't be anything else, not when his every move, each piercing word, was a calculated insult.

His gaze flicked to her lips. The pressure of his hand increased. He pressed closer, thigh to her thigh.

'I did no such thing.' Her voice was breathless, shameful evidence of weakness. 'I just arranged to marry.'

'Arranged to marry.' He shook his head. 'That's what you call it? You refuse me yet connive to wed another so you can deprive me of what is *mine*? Did you get a kick out of that, Alissa? You didn't just want the money, you also wanted to hurt me.' His voice thickened to a low, dangerous whisper that sent a chill of anxiety along her spine.

'It wasn't enough that you've lived a life of indulgent luxury at the expense of my family. That you had every opportunity our money could purchase.' His searing gaze didn't release hers. 'You squandered those opportunities.' His lips thinned into a disapproving line. 'What have you made of yourself? You have a dead-end job, a well-developed taste for parties and a criminal record.'

His disdain triggered a rush of desperate energy. Alissa lifted her hands to his shoulders and shoved, desperate for space. But he didn't budge. He was as immoveable as the island along which the car sped.

Impotent, she could only brace her arms, hoping to prevent him from closing the tiny gap between them.

'You're so sure of my guilt.' Her voice was overloud in the cocooned silence of their private compartment. 'Did it never occur to you I'm as much a victim in this as you?'

More so. For Dario Parisi had turned the situation to his own advantage with the sure, quick wit and daring of a natural predator. He was beyond her league in that and so many other ways. But she refused to be cowed.

'A victim?' His eyes roved over her, his stare so intense she felt it, like the slide of burning ice on skin.

Her lips tingled as if singed by fire when his gaze dropped to her mouth. For a heartbeat, for two, he stared. By the third pulse beat the tingle had become a throb. By the sixth her breathing had constricted, coming in short, hard pants that made her breasts rise and fall mere centimetres from the solid, imposing strength of his chest. By the ninth her lips felt tender, swollen, as if bruised by his ravaging look.

She tried and failed to forget the taste of his lips on hers. The blaze of heat that had engulfed her as he marked her with the brand of his possession. Though he didn't care for her, he'd taken the time to remind her she was his wife. His chattel.

And, despite every instinct for self-preservation, part of her responded to that primitive claim!

Still he didn't move. His sleek brows arrowed down in a frown of diabolical concentration. With his deep widow's peak, glossy dark hair and spare, powerful features he was the epitome of danger, his elegance a façade to raw power and primal urges.

His gaze held her immobile, in thrall to this thing that sparked between them. It was something she didn't want to name. Something that scared her more than threats or promises of reprisal.

He looked away and Alissa almost sobbed with relief.

Till he moved again. He cupped her face, his thumb on her mouth, pressing open her lips. Darts of fire shot out from his slow, deliberately erotic touch, straight to her engorged nipples and her belly.

Horrified, she stared into his darkening eyes.

She tasted his skin on her lips. A salty, musky tang. His thumb pressed lower, dragging her bottom lip down till he could invade her mouth, swiping her inner lip and tongue. That small invasion was shattering.

She read the glitter in his eyes, no longer cold and indifferent but febrile with an unholy pleasure. He knew exactly how devastating she found his caress.

His thumb traced the ridge of her teeth and her eyelids flickered, heavy with the weight of this new and alien force. She wanted to bite down on his flesh. Suckle it, draw it into her mouth, make his body heat and writhe like the twisting coils of sensation flaring inside her.

How had her anger morphed into this?

His lips drew back in a smile of stark masculine satisfaction. He closed in on her and she was helpless to break the spell of his touch and her own surging desire.

It was only as his head lowered, his chest brushing her oversensitive breasts, that she regained her sanity.

With both hands she clamped hold of his sinewy wrist and pulled. The silky hair below his cuff tickled but she ignored it, just as she ignored the frantic messages of her brain. Messages of thwarted desire and soul-swamping need.

Once she'd thought Dario less of a threat than her abusive grandfather. She'd been wrong. Dario had only to look at her, touch her, and she turned into someone she didn't know. Someone ravaged by disturbingly primal needs that Alissa Scott had never experienced.

'We may be married but you don't have the right to paw me,'

she gasped, thrusting his hand away and shoving at his chest. Beneath his open jacket she felt hard-packed muscle. Heat and power and pure male energy.

She shut her eyes and prayed this madness would cease.

'You give me the right when you look at me like that.' His uneven whisper was a rough growl. 'If ever a woman invited a man—'

'Enough!' Her eyes snapped open. 'Read my lips, Signor Parisi. I—do—not—want—you—near—me!' She punctuated each word with a thrust of her hands, becoming more desperate as he remained stolidly unmoving. She was at his mercy, locked in this tiny space.

Her heart hammered a panicked beat that threatened to choke her. Claustrophobia, the old enemy, engulfed her, making her senses swim and her head spin. The world closed in, darkening her vision to a narrowing tunnel of fear.

'Please,' it was a hoarse whisper, 'I...'

An instant later she was free. Cool air brushed her cheeks from an open window. Light banished the encroaching shadows. She slumped. Dario's stare raked her. But as she gulped down sweet air even that didn't matter.

She was safe. For now.

Dario scrutinised her intently, searching her pale features for signs of satisfaction or triumph. Her play on his sympathy had worked.

Was she so good an actress? He frowned, noting the pulse hammering in her slender throat. Her breathing was ragged, as if strained by fear.

Moments before she'd been caught in the same heady sizzle as he. With an expert knowledge honed over thirty-three years he'd recognised it. Despite her denials she'd been so hot and ready he could have had her on the back seat of the limo. Anticipation had thrummed through him.

At first he'd assumed it was a trick, seduction to soften him up for another attempt to wheedle cash from him.

Except she hadn't initiated that erotic little interlude. He had.

Now she gave an excellent imitation of a woman overcome by fear. Could he have so misread her? Had she truly been unwilling? The idea gnawed at his belly. He would never force himself on a woman in that way.

Or perhaps she was chagrined to find her fake response to him was the real thing?

Dario had no false modesty about his effect on women.

Now he was stunned at the sliver of doubt puncturing his certainty. He'd closed in on her out of anger, wanting to punish her. He hadn't forgiven her for making this difficult. She could so easily have agreed to his proposal years ago and all this would have been long settled.

Dario wasn't used to being manipulated. He'd been forced to barter his name to acquire the *castello*, marrying a Mangano. Yet when he'd finally swallowed his pride this woman had thrown his offer in his face. She'd tried to make a fool of him by ensuring he didn't get his inheritance. She'd even had the gall to ask for money up front before the wedding. As if he'd finance her lifestyle!

Now his plan to punish her had backfired. She'd brought him to a fever pitch of arousal in moments.

He'd barely touched her. Hadn't even kissed her. Yet the taste of her was imprinted on his palate. Their kiss yesterday had been a necessity then a punishment and then, to his astonishment, a pleasure.

One taste and he craved more.

Dario sank back, his mind whirling. Despite all he knew about Alissa Scott she'd got under his skin.

It was not to be tolerated!

The sight of familiar security gates eased the tension between ter blades. Soon he'd be home. This illusory link ould snap once he resumed his usual routine— ed as the car swung up the approach to the house. His gaze fixed on a cluster of people around a small figure in black at the foot of the entrance staircase.

Che diavolo! This was just what he'd hoped to avoid.

The car purred to a halt. Alissa looked out the window and gasped. She'd thought the end of this journey would bring some respite. How wrong she'd been.

Her eyes goggled as she took in the scene before her, lit by the setting sun. A masterpiece of minimalist architecture greeted her. Massive, soaring, stark white but for slender columns of polished steel and vast expanses of smoky glass wall. This couldn't be his house, surely?

Her gaze strayed from the huge bronze entrance doors, down the imposing steps to the group watching the car.

Alissa heard a burst of pungent Italian oaths that would have done her grandfather proud. Disconcerted, she slewed round to see Dario staring at his welcoming committee. The stern, lowered brow and the tight set of his jaw betrayed displeasure.

'Stay here!' he barked, then swung open the door and unfolded his length onto the driveway.

He stalked across the gravel and a resounding cheer echoed around him. He took the hands of a slight figure at the centre of the crowd. The woman was tiny but projected an air of authority. Alissa saw the woman's grey head nod as she broke from his grip, her hands gesticulating.

Abruptly the scene changed. Dario bent to kiss the woman on both cheeks, there was another cheer, then he strode back, his long legs eating up the distance.

There was no mistaking the grim annoyance in those grey eyes as he opened the door and held out his hand. His mouth was pinched in a straight line and his nostrils flared as if he took deep breaths to calm himself.

Reluctantly Alissa put her hand in his, and then almost withdrew it as a jangle of nerves cascaded up her arm and through her body. Her gaze flew to his, aghast, and she saw the almost imperceptible tensing of his jaw, the narrowing of his eyes that told her he felt it too—that instantaneous spark of connection.

'Come. There's someone waiting to meet you.' He tucked her arm in his, covering her fingers. She felt blanketed by his heat, yet she shivered. 'But take note.' His voice was a low, silky threat. 'Say as little as possible. You'll smile and nod and I'll do the talking. Understood?'

'Why?' Despite the exhaustion that made her sway on her feet, she had no intention of blindly kowtowing.

She caught his eye, hoping to look confident. Then she wished she hadn't. His look could freeze blood at fifty paces.

'Because if you don't, if you utter one word of disagreement, I'll make sure the next six months are the most miserable of your life. And that money you want from the estate? It might even be delayed.'

His voice was a lethal slash of sound. But worse was his expression. He wore a smile that from a distance must look charming. Up close it accentuated the feral anger in his eyes, the raw savagery of his tone. He looked like every nightmare her grandfather had ever conjured for her, evil intent cloaked by stunning good looks.

She could almost believe he'd like nothing better than an excuse to sink those strong white teeth into her tender flesh. Rapacious, fierce, deadly. That was Dario Parisi.

What had she got herself into?

'I...'

'Is that agreement? Speak up, woman.'

'Then stop looming over me!'

His eyes widened. Alissa even surprised herself. She'd thought she was too tired to meet his belligerence head-on, yet it wasn't in her nature to submit meekly to bullying. That was why she'd always been in trouble as a kid.

'Why can't you just *ask* me to cooperate?' She was sick of threats. Was that how all Sicilian men operated?

'Are you saying you would?' Disbelief coloured his voice. He didn't wait for her to respond. 'You will do as I say.' It was an order, not a question.

'Since you ask so nicely.' She pasted a sickly sweet smile on her face. Better than letting him see how his threat to withhold the money for Donna unnerved her.

'Good. Follow my lead like a good Sicilian wife and things will be easier for you.'

Alissa opened her mouth to snap out a retort. If there was one thing she'd never be, it was a good Sicilian wife!

He forestalled her by draping his arm around her, drawing her against his warm, solid body. That sucked the breath from her lungs and the words from her mouth. She hoped he couldn't feel her shiver. His ego was huge. Proof that she wasn't immune to him would only fuel his conceit.

'Come, *wife*, and meet your household.' His voice dripped an icy contempt that belied his wide smile.

There was a chef, a housekeeper, gardeners, a secretary, security men, maids and more. Names and faces blurred as Dario introduced her and good wishes were pressed upon them. The smiles looked genuine, as if they liked him. He must pay a fortune in wages. That was the only explanation.

'This is Signora Bruzzone.' His tone softened but his grip tightened. 'Caterina, this is my wife, Alissa.'

Alissa wondered if anyone else noticed him pause before the word 'wife'. But the woman before her gave no such indication. She drew Alissa out of Dario's grasp. His hands dropped reluctantly.

Gleaming dark eyes smiled up at Alissa as the older woman kissed her on both cheeks. She was grey-haired and dressed smartly in black. Her face was strong with character and traces of great beauty, her smile genuine.

Alissa, used to being on the small side of average, felt ungainly and ill-dressed beside her. The dark trousers, cream blouse and caramel jacket that had seemed perfect for travelling were rumpled now.

'Alissa, welcome to your new home!' Her English was accented but clear, her welcome genuine.

Alissa didn't know how to respond, especially with Dario glowering at her. Tentatively she returned the older woman's hug, uncomfortably aware of his scrutiny.

'Thank you, Signora Bruzzone.'

'You must call me Caterina. There's no need for formality. I was Dario's housekeeper for years and now I hope to be your friend.' The older woman smiled. 'You will be happy here. I know Dario will work hard to ensure it.'

Alissa struggled to repress a bubble of hysteria at the thought.

'As you say, Caterina, it will be my business to look after her.' His smooth tones slid along Alissa's nerves as his hand skimmed her waist. She drew in a trembling breath then bit down hard on her bottom lip, fighting the instinctive need to shrug him off and flee.

Snapping dark eyes surveyed her face then Caterina spoke again, more sharply this time.

'Dario! Look at the poor little one. She's exhausted. You shouldn't have subjected her to the long flight so soon after the wedding. Not everyone has your energy.'

The older woman smiled again. 'I have told him he should have waited and brought you here to marry. Then it wouldn't seem quite so strange to you.' Her eyes flashed a rueful glance over Alissa's shoulder. 'But it is always the way with this one. He sees what he wants and he is impatient. He would never take no for an answer.' She shook her head, but Alissa read fond approval in her eyes.

'Come. Everything has been prepared. I've seen to it myself. Welcome to your new home, my dear.'

Alissa opened her mouth to respond but the other woman gave an order to the staff, who separated, creating a pathway up the wide steps.

Without warning strong arms curved round Alissa's back and

legs. She was swung high, coming to rest against the hard heat of an impressive male chest.

'What…?'

Her eyes clashed with dark grey ones under straight black brows. The intensity of Dario's scrutiny cut off her question and her heart dived.

He stood unmoving, looking at her. She was insidiously aware of the feel of his powerful arms, of splayed hands pressed intimately against her. A hint of spicy scent made her nostrils quiver and somewhere deep inside a spark of something horribly like excitement fired her blood.

Dario's expression changed slowly. Shock sizzled in her veins as a real smile curved his sculpted lips. The effect on that chiselled, handsome face stole her breath.

He strode forward and around them cheers broke out.

He was halfway up the sprawling staircase before Alissa found her voice. 'I can walk. I'm not *that* tired.'

'It doesn't matter.' His words feathered her forehead. 'They'd be disappointed if we broke with tradition.'

'Tradition?' Alissa told herself it was weariness that dulled her brain. That her slow thinking had nothing to do with the effect of Dario Parisi's arms about her.

'Of course.' His teeth flashed a smile of genuine amusement, edged with something else she preferred not to identify. 'Didn't you know it's Italian tradition for a groom to carry his bride over the threshold?'

'You have to be kidding! You know this isn't—'

His embrace tightened and he strode faster, his long legs eating up the distance to the massive front doors.

'You and I know what our marriage is, but it does not suit me that anyone else should know.' He paused and looked down into her eyes. 'Welcome to my home, *wife*.'

Her breath hissed as he shouldered his way through the open door to the sound of raucous cheering from below.

'Well! Now you've kept up tradition you can put me down.' Her nerves were shredded. She needed space.

He shook his head and crossed a vast atrium towards a curving marble staircase.

'Ah, but that's not all. There's more.'

'More?'

'Oh, yes.' This time the smile he bestowed betrayed a raw heat that reminded her of a hungry predator. 'Didn't you hear Caterina? She has already made the preparations.'

'Preparations?' Alissa didn't like the look in his eyes, or the jerky way her pulse galloped in response.

'Of course. She has prepared our marriage bed.'

CHAPTER FIVE

ALISSA'S head swam as he strode through double doors and kicked them shut.

The room was huge, luxurious and private. The whisper of his breathing and the frantic thrum of her pulse were the only sounds.

A vast lake of smoky blue carpet spread like a reflection of the indigo sea beyond the enormous windows. The furnishings were few but impossibly expensive. The centrepiece was a bed: wide, low and far too large. It filled her vision and she couldn't look away.

Panic gripped her, fuelled by his menacing threats in the car, and more, the savage satisfaction she'd glimpsed in his eyes as he carried her up the stairs.

This man despised her, he couldn't possibly want...

'I'd like to stand on my own feet now,' she said as calmly as she could. 'There's no need to perform for your audience any more.'

'Ah, but you heard Caterina. You're exhausted.'

Alissa didn't look at him. She felt too vulnerable, here in his embrace. His searing gaze was too disturbing.

'Not that exhausted! Put me down. Now!' She welcomed the surge of anger. It beat the insidious chill of fear and the edgy awareness hands down.

Instead of answering he shifted his hold, drawing her closer, pacing slowly to the bed. Alissa's heart beat in time with each step as tension coiled tighter.

When he stopped the bed was an unending expanse below her. Blinding-white linen filled her vision, old linen, edged with ornate, handmade lace. The scent of lavender and sunshine emanated from it. Petals were strewn across the comforter. In the centre lay a plump, blush-pink rose.

'As you wish.' He lowered her.

Alissa was torn between wanting to tear herself from his arms and trying to scrabble back into them rather than be placed like some virgin sacrifice on his marriage bed.

The bedding cushioned her like an embrace. She held herself stiffly, sitting primly away from the luxuriously soft pillows.

'You can't mean for us to share this bed.'

'Why not?' His voice was a sultry murmur, his eyes glittering with a light she didn't want to decipher. 'We're man and wife. It *is* customary. Are you afraid there isn't room for two?'

Despite her best intentions, Alissa's gaze strayed over the bed. Its modern lines were designed for something less traditional than heirloom sheets. Satin perhaps, sinfully soft and caressing. She could imagine Dario sprawled here on black satin. Dario with a svelte, dark-haired beauty.

Alissa shot off the mattress, horrified at how vividly she pictured him naked. Her knees trembled as she faced him. He looked as implacable as a carved deity.

'Don't even joke about it, Signor Parisi. You and I both know you have no interest sharing this bed with me.' She refused to dwell on the possibility that she was wrong. 'I'm sick of your innuendoes and accusations. I'm tired after the trip and definitely not in the mood for your point-scoring games.'

Alissa breathed deep, trying to calm her racing pulse. She'd been on a roller-coaster ride of anxiety too long. She needed to claw back some control.

'Now,' she said, squaring up to his unreadable gaze, determined not to let him sense her fear, 'I've gone along with this charade and I haven't disappointed your fan club out there. I've been *more* than reasonable, putting up with your he-man routine carrying me up here.' She paused and dragged in another deep breath, wishing she could rid herself of the shivery awareness.

'I'd appreciate it if you'd show some courtesy and give me privacy. I don't care how you explain it to your retinue but we will *not* be sharing this bed.'

She spun round and marched to the far side of the room. With each step she expected the heavy weight of his hand to descend on her shoulder and halt her in her tracks.

Her fingers were unsteady as she pushed open a door and found what she'd hoped for: a bathroom. Relief flooded her as she entered and clicked the door shut, snapping it locked behind her.

For a moment she gazed at the palatial travertine and gleaming glass. Then she slumped against the door and let her shaky legs give way till she sat, huddled on the floor.

Six months of marriage. How was she going to survive?

Her situation got worse by the hour.

Dario stared at the door and willed his taut muscles to relax. His palms prickled at the memory of her curvaceous form in his embrace. Her rich, sweet fragrance lingered in his nostrils. More, his blood pooled and thickened low in his body.

Damnation! He was aroused. Fully, painfully aroused. By Alissa Scott, his not-so-convenient wife.

It had been the feel of her, warm and luscious and soft in his arms, that excited him. But even more, the sight of her standing up to him fearlessly when ninety-nine women out of a hundred would have meekly acquiesced.

The blaze of hauteur in her eyes as she called his bluff had been nothing short of magnificent. The belligerent jut of her chin, like an Amazon queen who didn't know the meaning of defeat. Her precise, cut-glass diction as she challenged him. The sizzle of defiance radiating off her. All had been superb. Glorious. *Sexy as hell.*

Even her dark red hair, tumbling around her shoulders as her rigidly upswept style disintegrated, had enhanced her splendour. It added a sensuous promise to her defiance. A reminder that beneath the glacial indignation every inch was warm, red-blooded woman.

The undercurrent of attraction had exploded into a tidal wave of wanting. He couldn't fathom it. He'd become accustomed to capitulation, not defiance. But this one woman, daring to confront him as no one had in years…

She'd been scintillatingly *alive*. Vibrant and real in a way few women were. She didn't simper or mindlessly agree or deliberately issue sultry invitations.

She hated him.

And he'd never been so turned on in his life.

The realisation was a shocking body blow.

She wasn't his type. She was everything he despised. She was his blood enemy. She was trouble with a capital T. She was nothing like the quiet, charming woman he planned to find and make his permanent wife.

Yet he was across the room, his hand on the bathroom doorknob, without any memory of deciding to follow her.

Horrified, he snatched back his hand and strode to the windows. The indigo waves, ceaselessly moving, reminded him of her. Of the way her brilliant gaze darkened as she faced him down.

He shoved his hands in his pockets and swung round, only to be confronted by the bed. Even now he saw her there, russet hair and pouting lips pure invitation against the pristine bedspread. Her full breasts rising and falling in her passion.

He'd wanted to push her back against the covers, cup that delicious flesh in his hands, taste her again on his tongue. Find release inside her.

But sex meant complications. He had enough experience of importunate ex-lovers to understand that. Sex with his wife…that would be a complication on a grand scale. Better to keep this strictly business.

Suddenly the idea of spending half a year under the same roof as Alissa didn't seem simple. Even in a separate room she'd be a distraction. Knowing she was here in his home would be a potent disturbance to his well-ordered life. His plan to make the next six months as difficult for her as possible was backfiring. He'd intended to enjoy her discomfort, enjoy making her pay just a little for the inconvenience she'd caused and the damage her family had done.

She was supposed to be at his mercy. Not the other way around.

Dario tightened his fists. Perhaps it was enough to have the *castello* in his grasp. He needn't sully himself with petty vengeance, despite the provocation.

He'd master this unwanted desire and forge ahead as he'd always done. Only his total-focus determination had got him where he was today, out of a nondescript orphanage and into the rich lists. If he'd let himself be sidetracked he'd still be nothing, nobody, not the worthy inheritor of his family pride and prestige.

He turned. His gaze flickered to the bathroom door but he headed for the landing. Alissa could wait. He had to straighten things out with Caterina. She was far more than his retired housekeeper. She was the one person who'd known him since those early days in the orphanage. She'd believed in him, giving up her job to keep house for him as his quest to rebuild the Parisi fortunes prospered.

He hadn't told her his plan to marry. His current housekeeper must have spilled the news so instead of arriving to see his new wife installed in an apartment of her own he'd been faced with Caterina's joyful excitement. She'd even made up a marriage bed with linens inherited from her grandmother.

He tunnelled a hand through his hair. Going through the farce of carrying his bride over the threshold had been easier than telling Caterina the truth.

She'd been at him so long to find a 'nice girl' and settle down. He hadn't had the heart to explain that this was all about business, property and a decades-old feud.

Now he'd have to. He squared his shoulders and strode out of the room. He ignored the small voice that warned his life, his foolproof plan to get everything he wanted, had suddenly become dangerously complicated.

It was the middle of the night when Alissa woke on the sofa in Dario's bedroom. She must have nodded off waiting for him to return. Jet lag and stress had exhausted her, yet she could scarcely believe she'd slept.

A blanket covered her and she was dressed but for her shoes. She darted a look at the massive bed.

It was empty. Her heartbeat notched up a pace when she saw it had been slept in. Where was he now? She sat up.

That was when she noticed the deep murmur. Not the sound of the sea—the roll of incoming waves was slower and more distant. She stared into the silver-grey moonlight, realising it was Dario she heard, his voice husky, rich and deeply male. It tingled across her senses like the prickle of approaching lightning, making her skin contract.

Alissa squirmed. She was too aware of the big, bothersome Sicilian. She tried to convince herself anxiety tensed her muscles but her restlessness had more to do with feminine awareness. It had been like that from the moment she met those clear-as-crystal eyes and felt a jolt like a fast-dropping elevator in the pit of her stomach.

If she could concentrate on Dario Parisi as her enemy she could fight him. But as she finally spied him, almost naked on the balcony, her determination to do just that slipped from her mind.

The moon revealed a sleek body of honed muscle, broad shoulders and long, taut limbs. Her breath stopped then escaped on a whoosh of desperation.

How did she fight the devil when he had the body of an angel?

He paced, talking into his phone. Each powerful stride revealed leashed energy and supreme fitness, as if he were an athlete impatient for his event. Even the shadow of dark boxer shorts low on his hips promoted the fantasy.

She caught one word, 'Maria', as he turned near the open glass door. His girlfriend? Was that why he was impatient? He was stuck here with a wife he didn't want when perhaps he'd rather be with Maria, working off some of that sizzling animal energy.

Alissa swung her legs to the ground, shoving aside the blanket and leaning her elbows on her knees. Nausea hit her at the idea of Dario and another woman.

It couldn't be jealousy. That was absurd. She didn't even like him. She wasn't attracted to that…master manipulator. The man who'd shown no compunction and every sign of chilly contempt as he bent her to his will.

'Ah, you're awake. My apologies if I disturbed you.'

He stood before her, legs planted wide and hands on hips in a stance that was purely male and appallingly attractive. The fact that he wore nothing but a pair of silky boxers and an enigmatic smile obviously didn't concern him in the slightest.

He was so supremely self-confident.

Every cell of her body clamoured to alert. Not with fear but with something far more dangerous.

Alissa jerked her gaze to his gleaming eyes, pretending she hadn't just imprinted a stunning picture of raw male beauty onto the dazzled lenses of her eyes.

She refused to be attracted to him. No matter what her body thought. Her mind was stronger.

Surely it was stronger.

'Why didn't you wake me?' Her voice, high and breathless, sounded like a stranger's.

'Why disturb you when you were comfortable?' His tone had a satisfied, unsettling edge.

'Don't play games, Dario.' She paused, astonished at the shot of pleasure that speared her at the sound of his name on her tongue. The enveloping darkness had altered the atmosphere between them. The very air felt charged. 'I didn't want to sleep here.'

He lifted his shoulders and, despite herself, Alissa was enthralled by the ripple of muscle and sinew on his lean, hard body. Moonlight lovingly silvered each taut curve and plane.

'As you fell asleep and refused to rouse, I assumed you weren't serious.'

'You tried to wake me?' Her mouth dried at the thought of those long fingers touching her while she slept. A tickle of sensation feathered her waist, her hip, as if in response to the light brush of a hand.

Was it possible he *desired* her? Had he wanted her awake to consummate their marriage? Anxiety and outrage flared. And a thrilling undercurrent she preferred to ignore.

He stepped close and her fingers curled into the sofa's fine leather. His gaze pierced her, as if he saw the weakness weighting her bones. She strove to look away, horrified at the drift of her thoughts. The tang of the sea on the breeze tickled her nostrils and the scent of warm skin mingled with it. She tugged the blanket over her knees, wishing for a more substantial barrier.

'You seem very much at home in my bedroom.' His voice was deeper than ever. A deliberate taunt. Alissa's eyes flickered to the wide bed. Even in this light she could make out a scattering of rose petals.

The marriage bed they were supposed to share.

The thought was unnerving. A traitorous part of her wondered how it would be sharing that space with this man—fit, strong and no doubt practised in every sensual skill.

Madness!

Yet she recalled the dreamy look on her mother's face years ago when she'd described meeting Alissa's father. Like a bolt of lightning, she'd said. So strong she hadn't hesitated to marry him weeks after they'd met.

Instant attraction was appallingly dangerous. Her mother

hadn't known what sort of man he really was. That he'd dump her just after the birth of their second child.

Alissa had more sense than to fall in love, especially with someone like Dario. But here in the warm night, where she felt the caress of his breath on her face, she wondered if women in her family had a predisposition to instant, all-consuming lust. To attraction that drove out logic.

Had that happened to her mother? Had Alissa inherited a terrible weakness for the wrong man?

No! It was a midnight fantasy, fuelled by anxiety. In the morning she'd feel nothing. She lifted her head and met the glitter of his eyes head-on.

'Don't get carried away by your ego, Signor Parisi. I was jet-lagged, that's all.' She busied herself, holding her breath while she folded the blanket. 'You can show me to my room now.'

He said nothing, just stood, arms akimbo, watching her. His eyes waited to trap her as she looked up. Once more she felt the shock of awareness shudder through her.

'I'll make a deal with you.' His voice was low and even. No sign that he felt anything except impatience. 'If you can live quietly for six months with no embarrassing scenes, no attempts to score points in front of others, I'll ensure you're comfortable till we inherit and divorce. You'll have the freedom of the estate and the local towns. I'll even provide a driver for you.'

Alissa stared, wishing the lights were on so she could fathom his expression.

'Why should you do that?'

He raised his shoulders and spread his hands palm upwards in a gesture that was pure Sicilian.

'A truce is easier for both of us.'

'What do you get out of it?' He wasn't obliged to provide anything but the roof over her head. After her grandfather's mean ways and a taste of Dario's dislike, she wouldn't have been surprised if he'd charged her board.

'Contrary to what you think, you're not my top priority.' His voice dipped into sarcasm. 'I have major commercial projects underway, more important things on my mind than continually sparring with a Mangano.'

'I'm not a—'

'No, how could I have forgotten?' The soft chill of his words stopped her. 'You're a Parisi now.'

It was true. For the next six months she was no longer Alissa Scott. The realisation unnerved her. As if in acquiring his name she'd somehow mislaid something of herself. Something vital.

'I'll never be a Parisi,' she said in a rush. 'I'm a wife on paper only, not your possession.'

Her fingers clenched. She'd had enough of men shoving her into moulds of their making, treating her as a chattel to be bartered and negotiated over, like a lifeless piece of property. His stare grazed her but she didn't look away.

'You're right,' he said at last. His husky voice rasped across her nerves. 'You'll never be a Parisi.'

Odd how his dismissal jarred. As if she cared what he thought, cared whether he believed her good enough to grace his oh-so-special family tree.

'But meanwhile you are my temporary wife. Why not accept my hospitality graciously? All I ask is that you behave with propriety.'

'Propriety?' Lava-hot anger coursed through her blood. She shot to her feet and paced away from him, needing an outlet for her simmering temper. 'What? No wild parties, you mean? No drugs?' She swung round to glare at him from the other end of the room. 'Is that what you're worried about? That I'll contaminate the illustrious Parisi name?'

His stillness told her that was exactly what he meant. Disappointment swamped her. Why was she surprised? He knew about her conviction. That she was intimately acquainted with the less salubrious entertainments awaiting young girls in a big city. She shuddered as she remembered those nightmare days.

'Don't sound disappointed, Alissa.' Her name in his mouth was a lethal weapon, carving through even her fury to burrow deep inside her flesh. A weak part of her responded even now to the sexy promise of this man.

She clenched her jaw, horrified to find she fought two enemies: Dario Parisi and herself. Never had she reacted like this to any man!

'Definitely no drugs,' he said. 'No wild parties.' He paused and she lifted her chin. 'But I was thinking more of romantic liaisons. You will not see other men while you are my wife.' His voice dropped to a rumble that reverberated across her skin. *His wife.* She rubbed her hands over her arms, smoothing away the sensation.

'Publicly we'll maintain the fiction of marriage but in reality we need have little to do with each other.' He paused. '*If* you can behave with decorum. And believe me, there will be people checking that you behave.'

Minders. Spies. He'd employ a private detective or body-guard to watch her every move. It was like the past all over again. But she sensed Dario Parisi's authority was even more potent than Gianfranco's had been.

For a moment the darkness pressed down on her, stifling, heavy, like a velvet weight that muffled the senses and impeded her breathing. Her chest tightened and blood rushed in her ears. Finally she forced down the welling void of fear.

'And you?' she said into the waiting silence. 'Will you also behave with decorum?'

'*Cosa?*'

She stalked towards him, anger driving her on. She revelled in it. Better that than fear. 'Will you give up your indulgences? Give up your women, your pleasures, so people believe we're married?'

Dario shifted his weight. He loomed taller, ominously threatening. Alissa stood her ground, noticing the sharp line of his jaw and the tendons taut in his neck.

'Careful, *cara*. It's dangerous to pick a fight with me.' His words were a whisper. 'Goad me too far and I may decide the best approach is to make this marriage real in every sense. Perhaps then you'll be more amenable.'

Time stood still as he held her gaze, letting his threat sink in. Her insides curled at the hint of anticipation in his tone. At the scent of sexual danger in the air. As if he'd like the excuse to seduce her. At this moment he might even succeed. Despite her fear and her wariness, she responded to him in the most appalling way.

'I just want to ensure you play your part in this charade.' Her voice wobbled.

Finally he nodded, a bare fraction of movement, and Alissa breathed again. 'For the next six months no one will have cause to think I'm interested in any other woman. They'll believe we're devoted.'

'That wasn't what I meant! You don't have to pretend we're…'

'Intimate?' Suddenly he was right there before her, filling her senses, invading her space.

Silently she nodded, fearful of the quicksand of hidden desires and emotions beneath her feet.

'Perhaps you're right. That would be too much.' Yet he didn't move, just stood, a living, breathing masterpiece of maleness. Alissa sucked in a deep breath then wished she hadn't. He smelt like sun shining on lemon groves, like the sea's salt spray, like hot sexy man.

She broke away, needing distance. 'So we behave impeccably and live separate lives?'

'Precisely. We'll need to be seen together sometimes. At civic receptions, that sort of thing. But that won't be often. You'll have your own rooms.'

Tendrils of relief spread and flowered inside her. 'Perfect. Why don't you show me now?'

'Your suite isn't ready. Tomorrow will be time enough.' For the first time his words were rushed, as if he was uncomfortable.

What was he hiding? Something about her room? That wasn't

likely. Or perhaps about the old lady, Caterina, who'd welcomed her so warmly and made up the marriage bed?

'You didn't tell her the truth, did you? Signora Bruzzone. You let her believe this marriage is real!'

Again he shrugged, but this time the movement was stiff, as if she'd hit a sore spot. 'It's only for one night. Tomorrow she'll be gone.'

Alissa stared, sensing his tension. Her mind whirled. Caterina thought they'd married for love. Had he withheld the truth because he didn't want to disappoint her? Because he cared for her good opinion? The knowledge stunned Alissa. Had Dario lied, sharing a room with a woman he distrusted, for Caterina's sake?

That made him suddenly...human. Flesh, blood and feelings. Warm, compassionate feelings, caring for someone else. This the man who'd chastised her for dressing as a bride so as not to disappoint her sister!

She stood still, stunned to realise his aloof exterior perhaps hid a chink of finer feeling. Who'd have guessed?

But why was he so sensitive of Caterina's good opinion? She was his ex-housekeeper, not his mother.

Suddenly Alissa realised the significance of that scene when they'd arrived. Not one member of Dario's family had been present. She frowned.

Had he fallen out with them all? It was odd, when he talked so much about family honour. Maybe his sense of honour was of the destructive variety, like her grandfather's.

'What are you doing?' she asked as he crossed to a set of doors on the other side of the room.

'Getting dressed.' He disappeared into a huge dressing room. 'You can spend the rest of the night here.'

When he emerged, he was dressed all in black. It suited him, far too much.

'I'll see you at breakfast. I have work to do.' He didn't even glance her way as he strode from the room.

Instantly Alissa felt that tiny spark of warmth vanish. She fooled herself if she believed he was motivated by anything other than self-interest.

Was he already breaking his promise to behave discreetly? Did his 'urgent work' go by the name of Maria?

Alissa grimaced as anger and nausea swamped her.

The suspicion that he'd gone to meet his lover in the night should be nothing to her. She should welcome his departure. So why did she feel sick at the thought of Dario spending the rest of the night in another woman's arms?

CHAPTER SIX

THE sound of feminine laughter on the sea breeze curled insidiously into Dario's consciousness. Evocative, familiar laughter. The sound of his wife enjoying herself.

Not that she laughed around him. Then she was stiff and careful, as distrustful as he of the undercurrent of desire that rippled, strong as the tide, between them.

His brows drew together. He had to concentrate on this contract. He jabbed a finger at a clause then slashed it out and scribbled his initials in the margin.

A murmur of voices from the garden replaced the laughter and the next clause blurred.

Who was it this time? In just a week his bride had charmed all the household staff. She'd even broken through the grim professional barrier of the security staff rostered to accompany her when she left the premises.

At the crackle of paper he looked down and smoothed the contract that had crumpled in his fist. It was impossible to work.

Grimly he faced the unpalatable truth: Alissa intruded into his thoughts too often. Each day he received a report on her activities. Even that, short and factual, tugged his mind away from important business.

She swam, explored the estate, visited quaint towns and took scenic boat trips. She had cooking lessons with his chef, shopped for souvenirs and spent evenings in her room. He didn't know whether to be pleased or annoyed that she'd done exactly as he'd demanded.

She'd behaved with perfect propriety. If you could call it propriety to charm every male she met!

When he worked at home, like today, her presence was everywhere. From the daisies in the hall where once there'd been formal floral arrangements, to the sound of her laughter, breathless and enticing, drifting inside.

He'd waited for her to step out of line, show her true colours. But she'd deprived him of that satisfaction.

He barely saw her, rarely spoke to her. Yet she haunted him. He dreamed of her as he tossed in his empty bed. He woke with the taste of her in his mouth, imagining her exotic lily scent on his sheets. Despite his attempts to ignore her, this attraction gnawed at him incessantly.

Dario looked at his white-knuckled fists, felt the heavy throb of frustration low in his body and wondered how he could go another twenty-five weeks without decent sleep. He wouldn't seek sexual relief elsewhere. Even though this marriage was just a convenient merger, he had more self-respect than that. And he couldn't sleep with his wife. Giving in to this desire would hand her power on a platter.

Which left him furious and frustrated. He never gave in to weakness, no matter what the provocation.

A gurgle of laughter interrupted his thoughts.

Dario shoved his chair back from the desk.

Alissa's smile faded as a *frisson* of awareness crept up her spine. It didn't take Giorgio's wide-eyed look or the sound of footsteps on the path behind her to let her know Dario was approaching.

That telltale tingle was enough. It never failed.

Time and again she'd felt that delicious shiver and found him watching. Usually he turned and left without a word and each time her gaze followed hungrily. She couldn't help it. There was something about Dario. Something she'd never experienced with any man. Something dark and strong and irresistible. She fought it with her mind but her body hadn't got the message. He was dangerous. Yet something stirred inside whenever he came near.

Even concern for Donna couldn't prevent Alissa's alarming reaction, especially since her worries had been allayed a little by regular phone calls and by knowing she'd get the money her sister needed.

With a smile for Giorgio she turned down the path to the sea. She'd reached the shade cast by a stand of pines when Dario's voice stopped her.

'Running away, Alissa?'

She froze, her hand on the railing at the top of the steps to the beach. He was close, his voice soft in her ears. Her body tensed in awful anticipation. She hated that he could do this to her. She avoided him when she could but her reaction to him had only intensified, like a blade honed keen to razor-sharpness.

'Why should I run? I haven't done anything wrong.'

She turned, grateful for the railing as her knees threatened to buckle. She'd grown accustomed to him in tailored suits that emphasised his suave leanness and complemented the strong contours of his face. But in jeans that hugged long, powerful thighs and a white shirt with the sleeves rolled to reveal sinewy, golden forearms, he was devastating.

Despair threatened. The craving grew stronger each time she saw him. She should hate him, and yet...

'Why indeed?' He frowned as he paced closer. 'Feeling guilty at being caught flirting with my gardener?'

'Flirting?' Alissa's eyes widened. 'All we did was chat! He was telling me about his daughters.'

She liked Dario's staff. She enjoyed their hospitality in introducing a newcomer to Sicily. What surprised her was their enthusiasm for Dario. Their loyalty and admiration went beyond lip-service. They genuinely liked and respected him. Just as Caterina Bruzzone's affection had been real. There'd been tears of happiness in the old lady's eyes as she wished them well when she left for her home on the mainland the day after Alissa's arrival.

The locals Alissa met were pleased when they discovered she was from the Parisi estate. Her husband was respected. People spoke of his generosity, his support for charities and his schemes to rejuvenate the region.

It was as if there were two different men—the chilling manipulator who'd turned her life upside down and the generous man, admired by all. The dichotomy only increased her wariness and confusion.

Did something in her bring out the worst in him? Whenever he drew near every instinct warned of peril. Yet even that couldn't douse the thrill she felt deep within when they were together.

'If you say so. I'm sure you found the subject fascinating.' Dario's eyes were dark as storm clouds as they raked her. She wished she'd worn something other than a short denim skirt and singlet top. Something more substantial so she couldn't feel his gaze on her. Armour perhaps. She clung to the railing, tilting her head to meet his stare, ignoring the way her nipples tightened. Hoping he hadn't noticed.

He stepped near and automatically she paced back, only to find her foot dangling in mid-air.

'Careful!' Strong hands encircled her arms and pulled her close. A shaft of heat scorched her as she inhaled the unique scent that was Dario. A second later he moved away to stand looking out to sea, as if the sight of her pained him. As if touching her contaminated him. Her heart squeezed in indignation and distress.

'You don't want to fall and break your leg. That would impair your activities.' His tone was sardonic.

'Activities?' Was he still worried she yearned for a wild nightlife with good-looking guys and designer drugs? Stupid how the idea hurt.

'Your swimming and sightseeing.'

'I see.' She stared at his grim profile. So her 'chauffeurs' had reported her movements. She'd suspected it but the confirmation disappointed her. He didn't trust her an inch. She felt hemmed in, restrictions binding her tight. She was in limbo, unable to get on with her life, forced to live here on sufferance. Try as she might she couldn't pretend this was a holiday.

'What do you want, Dario?' Steadfastly she ignored the tiny thrill that came from saying his name.

'Must I want something?' He slanted a look her way. The banked heat in his gaze stoked unwilling need deep inside her.

'Yes. You spend most of your time avoiding me like the plague.'

'Does that disappoint you, Alissa?' The devil was in his eyes and in that slow, provocative curl of his sensuous lips. She shivered, imagining she saw an answering flare of sexual interest in his expression. 'Would you rather I danced attendance on you?'

'I couldn't think of anything worse.' She crossed her arms tight over her chest, telling herself it was only half a lie. The thought of being with him filled her with excitement as well as trepidation. That worried her sick. If only she could detest him as thoroughly as she ought.

'As it happens I do have a reason for interrupting your morning—to tell you we're invited to a business reception. I assume you have something formal to wear.' His gaze skated down her bare legs as if the sight annoyed him.

'Do I have to go?' Just ten minutes in his company unnerved her. How would she survive an evening? The air zapped and crackled with the energy pulsing between them. Yet, she hated to admit it, she'd never felt more alive than when she sparred with him. It was scary.

'I told you we'd need to be seen together. If we don't go the curiosity of the Press will mean no more pleasant outings for you. We give them some pictures and we satisfy local interest. It will only take a few hours.' His eyes narrowed as if he read her turmoil. 'Don't worry, I'll look after you.'

Alissa couldn't think of anything calculated to disturb her more.

'What sort of clothes?' she said quickly. 'I haven't got a cocktail dress.' Her wardrobe wasn't extensive.

His brows climbed. 'I'll have one of my staff drive you to a suitable boutique. Aim for classy rather than provocative if you can.' Again his gaze dipped disapprovingly.

'Since you ask so nicely, I'll try.' Saccharine dripped from her tongue. She had a good mind to buy something outrageous to provoke him. But the thought of his gaze on exposed flesh deterred her.

'You do that.' He stared across the bay, obviously dismissing her. She'd turned to leave when his deep voice stopped her.

'You haven't been out to inspect the *castello* you'll inherit. Why?'

She swung round, her gaze following his to the grim, squarish castle of sand-coloured stone climbing up from the rocky headland at the end of the beach. It was forbidding with its turrets and crenellated walls.

'*That's* the *castello*?' It hadn't occurred to her. She'd expected something less mediaeval. Not a real castle. That explained Dario's autocratic attitude. If the place had been in Parisi hands for generations his family was local aristocracy. He'd be used to deference and immediate compliance with his wishes. No wonder she made him scowl when she refused to acquiesce to his every whim.

'That's the Castello Parisi. Home of my family.' His voice was rich with possessiveness and pride. Alissa watched his face set in determined lines.

But what fascinated her was the glimpse of raw emotion in his expression. His eyes held a yearning look she'd never noticed before. It surprised her. It made him appear almost... vulnerable.

Dario really had a passion for the place. This was deeply personal to him. It wasn't just about acquiring real estate. What did the *castello* mean to him?

From the look on Dario's face his determination was about far more than besting the Manganos. She couldn't imagine any property being so important she'd sell herself in marriage to acquire it.

Nothing was that important to her. Nothing except her family.

Alissa flicked a look at the modern masterpiece that was his current home. Despite its unusual style it was homey and comfortable by comparison.

'You don't mind living so close? Overlooking what your family once owned?'

'Mind?' He gave the villa a cursory glance. 'I built here so I could see my birthright every day till I possessed it.' There was a chilling hint of obsession in his voice.

'I suppose you spent time there as a child.' He'd have happy memories of it. Though the *castello* had belonged to her grandfather he'd left it empty—the perfect place for an adventurous boy to explore. The idea lessened the unnerving impact of Dario's absorbed stare.

Dario shook his head. 'I've never set foot inside, nor will I till it's mine.'

'But surely you lived somewhere close and—'

He swung round and his eyes, gleaming grey like the barrel of a gun, pinioned her. 'Didn't your grandfather tell you?' He paused as if waiting for her to respond. The intensity of his stare grazed her skin.

'No, I can see he didn't.' His brow puckered as he met her confused gaze. 'Strange. I thought he'd revel in the story.' Dario shrugged, turning towards the sea and the distant mainland. His broad shoulders hunched as if against a chill wind only he could feel.

Something about his stance made Alissa want to reach out to

him, despite the danger he embodied. He looked so solitary. Like a man in pain. Even his skin seemed taut, stretched across the angles of his face.

'I didn't grow up here.' He hefted a deep breath then another. His broad chest rose and fell but the tension in his corded muscles didn't slacken. She felt its echo in her own rigid limbs. 'I grew up over there, on the mainland.'

'Your family left Sicily?' That had never occurred to her. She knew Sicilians lived close to their roots, with generations staying in the same village. Her grandfather had only left because his nefarious practices made it too hot for him to stay. 'They haven't returned with you?'

'My family?' Dario's mouth twisted in a grimace that tugged at something inside her. 'I have no family. Not any more.' He flung out an arm towards the brooding castle. '*That* is all I have left of my family.'

Alissa opened her mouth to question him, but didn't get the chance as he swung round to face her. His eyes flashed with possessive fire.

'The *castello* belongs to me by birth, by right, by tradition.' His eyes narrowed and her pulse thundered as his hot gaze raked her. 'Now it's mine by marriage too.'

For a moment grey eyes meshed with blue, tension spiked between them like an arc of high-voltage energy. The air sizzled and her heart pounded.

Was he claiming the *castello* or her as well?

With a raw gasp Alissa spun round and stumbled up the path, uncaring what he thought of her sudden flight. He frightened her. He had the driven look of a man who didn't mind what rules he broke as long as he won. The sort of man she'd learned to fear and despise.

Yet there was something else in his eyes, some strong emotion that squeezed her chest tight just at the tiny glimpse of his passion. Was it pain? Grief? Regret?

She shook her head. Why go to such lengths to acquire a place he'd never set foot in? This wasn't about mere avarice, she understood that much at least. This was about something more fundamental.

What had he meant, that the *castello* was all he had of his family? Surely he exaggerated. She couldn't imagine a Sicilian with no family. More, she felt a dull ache of distress at the idea of anyone deprived of family. Her grandfather had been appalling but her sister meant everything to her.

Alissa catapulted to a stop just inside the house, her mind reeling. Trepidation shivered through her as she remembered Dario's steamy, proprietorial look. The look that curled her toes and stopped her breath.

She had an unnerving premonition her peaceful stay, safe from his attention, was going to end in calamity.

Alissa scooped the plastic bucket through wet sand and plonked it on the lopsided sandcastle. Giorgio's little girls, Anna and Maria, crowed with delight when she lifted the bucket, leaving a perfect round turret. The toddlers clambered close, their hands full of shiny pebbles and shells, ready to decorate it.

'Careful!' Alissa grabbed one of the twins as she wobbled and lost her footing. 'There you are, sweetheart.' She sat Anna before her so she could reach the tower.

Their chortles made her smile, especially when Maria turned and draped strands of seaweed over Alissa's hair.

'A mermaid, am I?'

'With that hair there's no doubt about it.' The deep voice rumbled out of nowhere, dragging her round to face the sea. Her breath slid out and for a moment she forgot to breathe.

'Dar-yo, Dar-yo.' The twins erupted into movement, wriggling to their feet with an urgency that spelled ruin for their sandcastle.

His stride was fluid. She watched the bunch and release of

muscles in his chest, abdomen and long legs as he cleared the waves. He wore low-slung swim shorts that revealed the perfect interplay of sinew and muscle. Each tiny movement mesmerised her, as if she'd never seen a man before.

She'd never seen one like Dario.

From his water-slick coal-black hair to the perfection of his body and the grin he directed at the girls hurtling towards him, he was breathtaking. The glint of water on his flesh gilded him in the early-morning light. He looked like a sea god, powerful and potent. Alissa's insides contracted in shivery delight just watching him.

Then he was on his knees, arms outstretched to the girls. 'You'll get wet,' he warned, but they catapulted into his arms, babbling in excitement.

Alissa sat back on her heels, stunned, as she absorbed the sight of Dario, who'd manipulated her so remorselessly, laughing with the children. Obviously they knew him well. He understood their lisping baby talk far better than she.

She blinked, remembering his ice-cold enmity in Melbourne, the contemptuous tone as he'd spoken of her family. She'd never have believed him capable of such unfettered joy or such patience as she saw now as the girls draped him with seaweed and shells.

'You must be a merman too,' she whispered, unthinking.

Instantly dark grey eyes met hers and heat throbbed between them, blocking out the sound of the girls' chatter. The world around her eclipsed into a void as the connection between them intensified. He hadn't done anything but look at her, yet his potent attraction tugged at her.

Abruptly Alissa turned away and her tension eased a fraction. She stumbled to her feet, brushing sand away.

'You're not going swimming, are you? There are strong currents.' His voice, with its husky edge, made her pause, but she didn't meet his eyes.

'No. I've just learned to wear a swimsuit when I'm here with the girls. I end up getting wet and sandy.'

Yet it wasn't the fine grit that bothered her now, it was the sensation of his eyes roving over her body in her violet Lycra one-piece. The swimsuit covered everything that ought to be covered but it fitted like a second skin. Flames licked her body as his intense gaze scorched her.

She shook her hair so it fell across her breasts then grabbed her sarong and tied it high, letting the fabric drape round her. Still he watched. That should bother her. But what she felt as she met his stare was more like triumph, like excitement.

What was happening to her?

He knew. The glitter in his eyes, the tight, knowing curve of his lips told her he understood completely.

But it couldn't be. It was impossible. She couldn't be susceptible to a man who embodied everything she most hated. He was power-hungry, ruthless, selfish.

Except now, with the girls, his arms curved protectively around them, his head bent to their chatter, he seemed like a different man altogether. A man of gentle, teasing humour and tenderness. A man who, despite his gruelling work schedule and his mega-millions, still had time to know and play with his gardener's young children. The sort who might even one day tempt her to shed her wariness and hurt and trust a man.

Dario was a puzzle. Whenever she thought she knew him he revealed a new facet that intrigued her.

'Come,' he said to the girls, getting to his feet and taking their hands, 'Alissa is waiting.'

She couldn't prevent the smile tugging her lips as she watched him: six feet plus of sheer masculine power, gently leading the chubby twins. There was seaweed in his hair and a large shell on the wide plane of one straight shoulder. A suspicious melting sensation squeezed her chest. Hurriedly she looked away, gathering buckets and spades.

'It's time we went. Breakfast will be ready.'

'You breakfast with Giorgio and his wife?'

'Do you object?' They lived on his estate, where his word was no doubt law. She glanced at the cottage up the hill. The friendship she'd found here meant a lot since she was cut off from her sister and home. It was a delight to spend time with Giorgio's family now and then and it felt good to help out, giving them a break from the girls' restless energy since they had a newborn to care for.

'If they wish to invite you into their home, that is a matter for them.'

Instantly defensive, Alissa thought she detected disapproval in his voice. Her spine stiffened and her chin lifted. For a few moments she'd forgotten his low opinion of her. Now that knowledge stabbed her through the middle.

'Don't let us hold you up.' She gestured in the direction of his villa. 'You've probably got early-morning meetings. I'll see the girls home.'

He stood motionless so long she thought he'd ignore her dismissal. Finally he hunkered down beside the girls and said something in the local dialect that made them burst into giggles.

'Enjoy your breakfast, Alissa.' His husky, deep voice swirled around her, making her skin prickle with unwanted awareness. Then he turned and walked away along the beach, his stride easy and assured, owner of all he surveyed. Despite her best intentions she followed every step, avidly drinking in the superb picture he made.

Grimly she warned herself to be sensible.

So he liked children.

So he was gorgeous.

So his smile made her heart flip over.

He'd never smile like that at her. Dario and she were destined to be enemies.

Pity they were also man and wife.

CHAPTER SEVEN

DARIO wrenched the tie from his throat and tossed it onto a chair. His cufflinks followed, then his shirt as he strode onto his private balcony. The sultry air was so still he could taste the impending storm on his tongue.

But it wasn't the weather that got under his skin. He'd been unable to concentrate all day and had come home early. All because of Alissa. He'd taken in barely one word in ten at his meetings. His mind had been fixed on the woman who kept him awake night after night. His wife.

He couldn't shake the images of her on the beach today. Skin lustrous as pearls. Hair seductive fire, spilling round her. Body all feminine curves, lusciously rounded at hips and breasts yet such a tiny waist.

More, he grappled with the shock of seeing her happy and carefree with Anna and Maria. He'd pegged her as a woman who'd have no time for children. Yet she'd been careful of them, joining their fun while keeping a watchful eye on them. Her pleasure had been genuine and the sight of her had stopped him in his tracks as he emerged from his swim.

His body had responded predictably to the picture she made: a sexy, gorgeous, half-naked woman in the role of nurturer. Grimly he'd realised nothing could appeal more to a man's most basic instinct: to mate.

Meanwhile he struggled to adjust his assessment of her. This woman was more complex than he'd first thought. Dangerously complex. Something about her made him yearn for things he couldn't quite grasp. Yearn for things other than the carefully orchestrated future he'd set as his goal a lifetime ago to fill the yawning void in his life.

He tunnelled a hand through his hair, noting the encroaching storm clouds. A flash of white out to sea snagged his attention. Someone was out on a sea kayak. Someone in a white shirt with dark red hair. Too far out, with this storm coming in so fast. The bay grew dangerous when the wind was up, a lethal trap for the unwary.

Seconds later Dario was racing to the beach.

Alissa clung to the kayak, straining to drag herself up. But the strength had seeped from her arms. They were like jelly. She'd ventured too far out, only realising it was time to turn around when the rumble of thunder alerted her to changing weather. She'd raced back as fast as she could, but she'd grown exhausted as she struggled against unfamiliar currents and the suddenly massive sea.

A freak wave had toppled her over. Now all she could do was hang on. Fear swamped her but she refused to give in to it, despite the lashing spray that bit her skin and the surge that tossed her like flotsam. So long as she held on she had a chance. But her numb fingers were loosening.

A movement made her yelp as something slid against her. Were there sharks? Panic swelled and she swallowed water, half submerged beneath the waves.

Something hard encircled her arm, biting into her frozen flesh. It pulled and she came up for air, spluttering and gasping. Her heart was ready to burst and her lungs worked like bellows to draw in oxygen.

Swearing. She heard swearing. In Italian. Her befuddled brain barely took that in before she was grabbed beneath the arms and hauled from the sea.

'Hang on tight,' a barely audible voice instructed over the roar of the sea.

Dario. She recognised that husky-edged growl, even through the sound of the storm. She felt warmth beneath her and realised she was lying across his legs. He'd climbed onto the kayak and dragged her up too.

Relief swelled as she clutched his solid body. She'd be safe now. She couldn't imagine anything defeating him. If any man could battle the elements and win it was Dario. His determination, his sheer strength, would see them through. Besides, imagine his temper if she drowned before they inherited his precious *castello*!

It was the cessation of noise that roused her. The storm's full-throated roar died to a muffled rumble. The needles of rain on her skin stopped abruptly. Alissa's eyes fluttered open to an awareness of being held against something hot and solid. She nuzzled her head against her makeshift pillow and heard the steady thud of a heartbeat.

Dario! For a moment she allowed herself the luxury of sinking against him. Any longer would be dangerous.

'You can put me down.' Her voice cracked.

'Why, so you can run off and do something equally stupid?' he growled. His grip tightened. She looked up to see his chin jutting above her like the prow of a warship.

'I'm sorry. I didn't realise how fast the storm was coming in.' Remembered fear choked her throat and she bit her unsteady lip as he lowered her onto a fabric-covered surface. She blinked and looked around the gloomy interior. They were in the boat shed, jet skis and other craft stored around them. Alissa looked down to discover he'd sat her on a canvas day bed.

'Here.' Thick towelling draped her shoulders and strong hands rubbed her back, her hair, her arms. Slowly she felt the blood circulate, tingling through her body.

'I'm sorry,' she mumbled again. 'I didn't mean to put you in danger.'

'Me!' The towel was stripped away to reveal him full square before her, feet planted wide, like a warrior ready for battle. This warrior wore nothing but saturated boxer shorts and a gold watch. His chest heaved—with emotion, she suspected, rather than exertion. His glare could cut solid rock. Right now it sliced into her.

Alissa tugged the massive towel round her shoulders, her movements weak and uncoordinated after her desperate exertions. She tried not to feel intimidated by the blast of anger and undiluted testosterone he projected.

'You're worried about *me*?' His voice rose incredulously. 'Didn't I say the bay had dangerous currents? Didn't you see the storm approaching?'

She shook her head, feeling every kind of fool for putting herself in a situation where she needed rescuing. She'd been so distracted by thoughts of Dario, trying to make sense of the complex man and his motivations, she'd forgotten basic safety precautions like checking her distance from the shore.

'I apologise.'

'You apologise!' His voice was like thunder, welling around them. 'You could have been killed.' His hands were bulging fists, the muscles bunching ominously in his arms. 'Do you have any notion how close you came to drowning?'

Alissa didn't feel safe any more. The fury in his tone sparked recognition. A lifetime's lessons in violence stiffened her sinews. She scented the anger on his skin and instinctively she slid along the day bed, out of his reach. She swung her legs to the floor and forced herself to stand. She swayed but held herself upright with one hand clutching the metal bed frame.

'What are you doing, woman?' His forehead pleated, dark brows jamming together. 'Sit down before you fall!'

Dumbly she shook her head, her eyes never leaving his. She

didn't have the strength to run. All she could do was try to anticipate his first move.

He strode forward and fear clawed up through her chest. But instead of raising his hand he grabbed her and dragged her hard against his chest. His heart slammed a rough tattoo against hers as he lifted her off her feet.

'You have to be the most obstinate, difficult woman—'

The accusation ended as he bent his head and took her mouth in a plundering, voracious kiss that drew her into a storm of unrepentant desire. He swallowed her instinctive protest, clasping her close to his slippery body.

Shock held her immobile. In that instant before she could gather her wits he vanquished her incipient protest as his mouth softened. Now his lips and tongue caressed, invited, tempted. One hand slid down to cup her bottom and draw her close to the hard urgency of his body.

Excitement shivered through her. Sweet desire. Need. Her exhaustion was forgotten as she drank in his kisses, returning them with an untutored fervour that would have astonished her if she'd been capable of thought.

Nothing was real but this. His body straining urgently against hers. His mouth an instrument of pleasure. She cupped his jaw in her hands and felt a thrill of delight as this powerful man shuddered against her.

What was he doing? From somewhere a shard of reason pierced his non-functioning brain.

Alissa suffered from shock and exposure. She'd almost lost her life in the sea. The damnable treacherous sea that had been his enemy for so long. It had stolen everything that mattered to him. Everyone.

His arms tightened instinctively around her.

Was it any wonder he shunned love in favour of the future he planned, with a carefully considered marriage to an appropriate woman? No more emotional relationships for him. No love. Not when soul-destroying loss was the cost. Not when happiness was so easily wrenched away by greedy waves.

The sight of Alissa battling to stay afloat had brought back too many tragic memories. His heart squeezed as he realised he'd almost lost her too.

Finally he found the strength to lift his head, dragging raw breaths into his labouring lungs.

Dazed azure eyes stared up at him. Her lips were ruby-red and plump from his kisses. Hectic colour streaked her cheekbones, testament to the sudden passion between them.

What sort of man was he, letting emotions drive him to such lengths? His fury resulted from their near-death experience. Was that the cause of this almost unstoppable desire too? And the fear that made his heart clatter against his ribs?

He felt…he felt…too much.

Shame washed through him. She was traumatised. He had no right to treat her like this.

More, now that he knew her a little better he began to doubt his first assessment of her. What he'd discovered he admired. His instinct was to protect her.

He swung her up in his arms, noticing with grim pleasure the way her hands automatically rose to link at the back of his neck.

'Come on, Alissa. It's time a doctor checked you out.'

Five days later Alissa stood beside her husband at a reception in a magnificent old *palazzo* and tried to understand the change between them. There'd been no mention of that passionate kiss, no reference to the rescue, yet since that day Dario's attitude had altered. He didn't avoid her as much. Nor had there been more barbed remarks. They lived a wary truce.

Sometimes she looked into his eyes and glimpsed a flash of the incandescent fire that had almost consumed her that day in the boathouse. The fire that, to her shame, she couldn't help but miss.

Whatever Dario felt, he kept it to himself.

So much about the man she'd married was inexplicable, from his obsession with regaining the old estate to his fiery passion and his sudden withdrawal. She longed to ask about his family, hoping he'd exaggerated about having none. But she hadn't found the nerve to query him. Then there was the esteem in which he was held locally, his comfortable relationship with Anna and Maria—more like a kind uncle than a world-weary tycoon.

He'd flummoxed her the day of her rescue. She'd seen his simmering fury and smelt his anger with the preternatural awareness of an animal hunted by a predator. She knew the signs of untrammelled anger since she'd lived most of her life with its violent consequences. But, despite his wrath, he hadn't taken out his temper on her. Instead he'd given her the sweetest, most desperate kiss she'd ever known. One that left her wanting more.

Now tonight, the goalposts had shifted again.

Dario went out of his way to touch her, keeping her close as they circulated through the throng of dignitaries. His arm at her waist was possessive. The feather-light weight of his breath on her hair and cheek was a stealthy caress. His husky voice was intimate, binding her to him with invisible ties.

The intimacy was for public show. Yet that didn't prevent the warmth spreading and sizzling under her skin.

Her face ached from plastering on a smile. Her body was stiff from trying to maintain a distance between them. It was a losing battle. That casual drape of his arm tightened whenever she prised herself away a fraction.

She'd known he had a way with women and the looks that followed him round the room proved it. Yet it wasn't the young and lovely who received the full blast of his attentive smiles. The smiling, elegant pair they'd just left were in their seventies at least.

Dario was no longer the man she knew and distrusted. That unnerved her.

'You said we had to be seen together,' she whispered, 'not that we'd be like conjoined twins the whole evening.'

'Don't worry, Alissa. No one will mistake us for siblings.' His long fingers stroked the dark velvet at her waist and she sucked in a shocked breath. Such a tiny movement yet waves of pleasure radiated from his touch.

'Now we've been seen and congratulated, perhaps we can leave?' She stood rigid, locking her knees against the melting sensation that made her legs wobble as his hand idly circled.

His arm dropped. Instantly she felt bereft.

'No. I still have people to see.' His expression was suddenly grim. Had she annoyed him? 'If you would prefer not to accompany me…'

'Yes.' She sounded far too eager. 'I'd prefer.'

With a nod and a narrowing glance he turned and headed through the crowd. Alissa released her breath on a sigh. When she was with Dario she felt so unsettled. Even now she couldn't tear her eyes from him. Yet it wasn't distrust that kept her attention locked on him.

It was something more primal. More personal.

Her pulse revved as he turned and smiled at someone. His spare, sculpted good looks, his dark colouring might have been the inspiration for whoever invented the tuxedo. Surely no man had ever looked more elegant, more handsome, more dangerously powerful in such formal attire.

'Your husband is very handsome, Signora Parisi.'

Alissa blinked and looked up into the face of a gorgeous, elegant woman. Golden hair, stunning face. Eyes that were sharply assessing.

'Thank you, Signorina…?'

'Cipriani. Bianca Cipriani.' She paused. 'Your husband has a reputation for being ruthless. Many women would think twice before marrying such a man.'

Alissa caught her breath. This woman was trouble, that was obvious. But how to escape her without making a scene?

FREE BOOKS OFFER

To get you started, we'll send you
2 FREE books and a **FREE** gift

- -

There's no catch, everything is **FREE**

Accepting your 2 **FREE** books and **FREE** mystery gift
places you under no obligation to buy anything.

Be part of the Mills & Boon® Book Club™ and receive your favourite
Series books up to 2 months before they are in the shops and delivered
straight to your door. Plus, enjoy a wide range of **EXCLUSIVE** benefits!

- Best new women's fiction – delivered right to
  your door with FREE P&P

- Avoid disappointment – get your books up to
  2 months before they are in the shops

- No contract – no obligation to buy

2 **FREE** books
and a
FREE gift

We hope that after receiving your free books you'll
want to remain a member. But the choice is yours.
So why not give us a go? You'll be glad you did!

Visit **millsandboon.co.uk** to stay up to date
with offers and to sign-up for our newsletter

P9EI

Mrs/Miss/Ms/Mr _____ Initials _____

BLOCK CAPITALS PLEASE

Surname _____

Address _____

_____

Postcode _____

Email _____

MILLS & BOON®
Pure reading pleasure

The Mills & Boon® Book Club™ — Here's how it works:

Accepting your free books places you under no obligation to buy anything. You may keep the books and gift and return the despatch note marked "cancel." If we do not hear from you, about a month later we'll send you 6 brand new books and invoice you just £2.99* each. That's the complete price — there is no extra charge for postage and packing. You may cancel at any time, otherwise every month we'll send you 6 more books, which you may either purchase or return to us — the choice is yours.

*Terms and prices subject to change without notice.

MILLS & BOON®
Book Club

FREE BOOK OFFER
FREEPOST CN81
**CROYDON
CR9 3WZ**

NO STAMP
NECESSARY
IF POSTED IN
THE U.K. OR N.I.

'All successful entrepreneurs are single-minded.'

'But Dario is in a class alone when it comes to getting his own way, no matter the cost.'

'What is it you want?' Better to get this over quickly. She didn't want a scene with a jealous ex-lover.

'Just to give a friendly warning.' The blonde's eyes narrowed. 'If you're wise you won't trust him with anything you value, like your heart or your life. He cares for nothing but his precious Parisi estate.'

'Is that what happened to you?' Despite her better judgement Alissa couldn't quash the need to know.

'Me?' Bianca laughed. 'Hardly. *That's* the sort of woman your husband has always preferred.' With a leaden sensation in her stomach Alissa followed her gesture.

There was Dario, in intimate conversation with a gorgeous brunette. The woman looked like a model: tall, slim, with an air of fashionable languor and the serene face of a madonna. In her gown of silver gauze she was the perfect foil for Dario's dark suit and lean good looks. He stood close, his body language proclaiming his interest.

Bile rose in Alissa's throat. She pressed a palm to her roiling stomach. The sight of Dario, fascinated by the dark-haired beauty, made her nauseous. Her breath shallowed, her hands grew clammy.

These last weeks he'd sneaked under her defences, shattered her preconceived notions and made her doubt what she knew of him. More, he'd given her a taste of passion and foolishly she craved more. She was jealous of the brunette who so obviously intrigued him.

'Are you all right?' Bianca's words dragged her from her horrified stupor. 'You're very pale.'

'I'm OK.' Alissa turned her back on the perfect couple. She crushed stupid regret that she'd never be tall and glamorous, the sort of woman Dario found attractive.

She should thank her lucky stars! An intimate relationship with him would be disastrous.

'Why do you hate him?'

The other woman straightened. 'He killed my father.'

'He *what*?' She searched Bianca's face but she looked utterly genuine. A chill slid through Alissa.

'My father owned a company that once belonged to the Parisis. Dario was obsessed with acquiring it and everything else in the old Parisi estate.' Her gaze flickered to Alissa. 'When my father refused his offers Dario used other means to acquire it.'

'What do you mean?' The hairs stood up on the back of Alissa's neck.

Bianca shrugged. 'Your husband is powerful. Suddenly there were problems on site, loan extensions cancelled. Pressure mounted from all sides. What was once a thriving business was re-assessed at a fraction of its value. My father had to sell but he got a pittance for it. He felt he'd failed us. That's when he took his life.'

Dario's skin prickled, senses alert as he felt her eyes on him. After weeks of repressed desire he recognised this heightened awareness instantly.

Casually he turned. Their gazes connected and his heart accelerated. He took in her creamy skin, the swell of her breasts beneath the square neck of her black velvet dress. She wore no jewellery, but with her sapphire eyes and fiery hair she needed no adornment. Her dress clung to her curves but was puritanical in its simplicity. Perversely it made him more eager to remove it. Her legs in sheer stockings and high heels were incredibly sexy.

It took a moment to notice the woman beside her. Bianca Cipriani. Was she dripping poison into Alissa's ears? Dario was surprised to find he wished the two women hadn't met. As if he cared for his wife's good opinion.

'Dario, are you listening?' His companion pouted. Automatically he apologised, realising he'd barely listened to her

chatter. Dario frowned. For months he'd considered her a con-
tender for the position of permanent wife after Alissa left. She
was sophisticated yet eager to accord with his wishes. She had
breeding, beauty, brains. She wanted children. She was Sicilian.
She was perfect for the role.

And yet... His gaze strayed to Alissa, demurely dressed to
kill. His temperature rose and his groin tightened. It annoyed him
to find he was more interested in his unwanted wife. He excused
himself and went to fetch her.

She stood alone now. Her eyes were a blaze of colour, lips a
plump, perfect invitation, at odds with her rigid posture. Tension
stiffened his every muscle and sinew as he approached.
Anticipation weighted his limbs, stirred his pulse to a heavy,
needy throb.

Tonight. He'd deal with this tonight, he decided as their eyes
locked and fire scorched his blood. He'd spent weeks pretending abstinence could master this unwanted desire. The time for
denial had passed.

He'd do whatever it took to get her out of his system for good.

CHAPTER EIGHT

'SIGNORA PARISI. There was a long-distance call for you. A message to ring your sister.'

Instantly the low-level anxiety Alissa had lived with for so long rocketed to the surface, morphing into fear. Donna had been fine last night, or so she'd said. Had something changed?

'Thank you.' She nodded to the housekeeper and hurried towards the stairs.

'Alissa.' Dario's voice, low and resonant, made her pause. Even through her worry the sound of his husky, deep tone could stop her in her tracks.

'Yes?' She turned but didn't meet his eyes. She didn't need that challenge.

'We need to talk. When you've made your call I'll be in my study, waiting.'

Startled, she looked straight at him but couldn't read his impassive expression. He had the face of a poker player. Of a man who wheeled and dealt in multi-million-dollar enterprises. And yet…there was something about the way he held himself, like a predator waiting to pounce,…

A tremor rippled through her. No! She was being fanciful. Worry over Donna made her imagine things.

'All right.' She turned and headed for her room, praying with each step that bad news wasn't waiting.

* * *

Dario poured himself a single malt, and then, in a move unusual for him, another.

The potent alcohol did nothing to soothe his tension. He was wound too tight, his body burning up with a hunger so rampant he felt like a raw adolescent. Except this attraction was nothing like the spike of physical desire he'd experienced as a callow youth. This was more intense, more disturbing, an omnipresent awareness that hijacked his mind as well as torturing his body.

It was enough to make him question his judgement. He wanted to believe she was all she seemed, feisty yet sweet, innocent even. Yet he had proof enough of her wild ways, her reckless carnal pleasures. She'd tried to steal his birthright, refusing his generous offers while conniving to wed another. She'd acted as his enemy.

Frustration and anger hummed through him. These growing doubts weren't like him.

He'd had his fill of decadent socialites. Of shallowness and avarice. Yet his gut instinct urged him to believe in her. More, something about her tugged at emotions he'd almost forgotten. That made him vulnerable.

He burned at the thought of her sharing her favours with other men. He couldn't repress a surge of jealousy at the memory of her ex-lover, Jason Donnelly. Dario's yearning made a mockery of his pride and his standards.

He swallowed the last of his Scotch, barely noticing it burn his throat. He poured himself another, furious that with her alone his formidable control was nonexistent. Just the sound of her voice, a whisper of her scent on the air and his mind blanked. His hands shook as he poured the whisky. Savagely he swore. He *would* conquer this weakness.

A breath of air feathered the back of his neck as the study door opened. It couldn't be reaction to her presence. No woman had that sort of power over him.

He turned. She stood inside the closed door, silhouetted by lamplight that caressed each dip and swell of her hourglass figure. His throat tightened as need, instantaneous and all-consuming, devoured him.

God, how he wanted her!

He'd expected her to flaunt her abundant charms. Instead she'd tortured him in a dress that covered her arms, her shoulders, her thighs. It should have been demure. But, in a devious twist of feminine power, that hint of cleavage and the way the fabric wrapped itself round her like a lover's caress turned demure into sinfully sexy.

'Dario, we need to talk.' His jaw tightened. The sound of his name in that breathless voice made him hard.

'Precisely what I had in mind. Drink?'

'No, thank you.' She walked further into the room and he read determination blazing in her eyes. Her posture was rigidly perfect. His wife had something on her mind.

Something in her set face tripped his internal alarm system. Something not quite right. Instantly he was alert.

There was nothing warm about her expression. Dario felt his ardour cool as his mind clicked into gear. Part of him loathed the suspicion but it rose with devastating inevitability.

Would this be the moment she showed her true colours? When she tried to persuade him to alter their agreement? Would she again try milking him for the wealth she'd grown accustomed to and now missed? From the moment she'd signed the prenuptial agreement along with the notice of intention to marry, he'd wondered.

Something stirred deep in his belly. Disappointment?

'I want to renegotiate our arrangement.' Her look seemed direct, honest and just a hint wary.

The stupid, fragile hope that he'd been wrong died instantly, leaving a queer hollowness in its place.

'There's nothing to renegotiate. When we inherit I'll organise the divorce and your payment.'

She stepped closer and he got the full impact of that wide-eyed look. For all his cynicism he melted a little under her soulful gaze. That stirred his resentment. He didn't take kindly to being played. He'd long ago developed armour against the wiles of avaricious women.

'Something important has come up.' She drew a slow breath, a predictable feminine ploy but effective. His gaze slid down to her full breasts.

'Really?' He kept his tone noncommittal.

'Yes.' She paused, as if hesitant. 'I need money now. The money from the sale of the *castello*. So I thought…'

What? That he'd give it to her? He owed her nothing. To the contrary, she'd grown up with the fortune and opportunities that should have been his. His fingers wrapped tighter round the glass as the old wrath took hold. He'd almost forgotten it these past weeks as he'd let her lull him into half believing he'd got her wrong.

Had that touching scene on the beach with the girls been window-dressing? Part of an elaborate ploy to allay his suspicions? Women had gone to greater lengths before now to win his attention. Could he have been that gullible?

No one made a fool of Dario Parisi.

'We could sign an agreement, a contract. I'll agree to sell you my share of the estate when we inherit and in return you give me my share of its value now.'

Dario shouldn't be surprised, yet the sour tang of disappointment filled his mouth.

'That's not possible.' He downed his whisky. The blaze of heat rocketing down his throat couldn't rival the flare of anger in his belly. Anger at himself for ever thinking he'd been wrong about her. Fury with her for not being what he'd hoped.

'Of course it's possible.' She paced closer and her scent, like an invitation to paradise, filled his senses. 'Your lawyers could draw up such a document.'

'I've no doubt you're right. But what good would it be when there's no guarantee I'd ever own the estate?'

'I don't follow you.' She tilted her head, the picture of innocent confusion.

'It's simple, *moglie mia*. Once you have my money, what's to stop you leaving?' For a moment an image of Alissa, shackled to his bed, wearing nothing but a beckoning smile, distracted him. Heat twisted in his gut. It would be one way of keeping his wife close. Pity he was supposed to be an enlightened twenty-first-century man.

'You'd have our contract.'

'Much good that would do when you desert me. I can't claim the estate unless we live together for six months.'

She spread her hands, palm up. 'But that wouldn't change. Don't you see? I'd stay here. The only difference would be that I'd have my share a little early.'

'A little?' He tilted a derisory brow. 'More than a little. Besides, I'd have no guarantee you'd remain.'

'You'd have my word. And a contract.' She approached and his body stirred.

'Contracts can be broken. So can promises.' He put his glass down. He had to steel himself against the shudder of need that ripped through him as he looked down at her. Even now, when she tried to squeeze cash out of him, the hunger didn't abate. What would it take to exorcise this woman?

'But…this is important!'

'I've no doubt you think so—'

'It *is*. Really.' Her fingers touched his sleeve, then she jerked her hand away as if she too felt the jag of electricity that sparked from the point of contact.

He'd never known such awareness.

'It's not for me.' Her voice was urgent, her eyes pleading. She raised her clasped hands to her breasts and he felt a primitive surge of satisfaction at the picture she made. The beautiful woman poised as a suppliant.

He wondered how it would be to have her beg him, not for

money, but for pleasure. For the release and ecstasy he could give her. Heat steamed off his skin as dangerous excitement scored his soul.

'It's for someone else.' She paused and he watched her hands clench tight against her breast. 'You don't know about my sister—'

'I do know. I made it my business to know.' He watched her eyes widen. 'Donna. Younger and with your colouring. Left school early. Recently married.'

Her eyes widened. Obviously she hadn't expected him to be so well acquainted with her circumstances, despite the background check he'd ordered.

'That's right.' She licked her lips with a delicate pink tongue and Dario almost groaned. Another blatant tactic, yet he wasn't immune.

She baited him, deliberately torturing him in the hope he'd weaken. Her tactics were so obvious they should be amusing. Except they worked. His libido roared into rampant life as he watched her.

'Well, it's for Donna. She needs money, a lot of it.'

His raised palm stopped her. He'd been angry before. Now fury hummed through him. She dared use her sister as an excuse for her greed? Only someone like him, who no longer had a family, could appreciate the depths she'd sunk to with this despicable lie.

She didn't appreciate what she had. She didn't deserve it.

Dario recalled the private investigator's report. Her precious sister had been found nightclubbing while under age, including the night of Alissa's drug bust. Now this woman had the temerity to paint herself in the role of caring older sibling! She hadn't been a decent role model when her teenage sister needed her. Any normal woman would have protected the girl, not led her astray.

'What's that to do with me?'

'You have money. Plenty of it. And Donna needs this cash desperately.' Her wide eyes looked so innocent even now he felt a tremor of response. Damn her.

'I know all about her need for money,' he said slowly, remembering the rest of the investigator's report. The younger woman had married a cattle farmer in the middle of one of the worst recorded droughts. The bank held an enormous mortgage over their heads. But he knew there was no danger of foreclosure. The drought had broken while he was in Australia. The bank wouldn't call in debts now there was every sign of a bumper year to come.

No, Alissa was using this as an excuse.

'You do? You've known all this time?' Eyes dark as the sea met his.

He nodded. 'I've read a comprehensive dossier on you and your family, remember?'

She stared silently, her face curiously blank, as if from shock.

'Well, then.' Her voice trembled a fraction. She really was a talented actress. 'You understand why I need to get hold of this money as soon as possible.'

'Then by all means find a way to help her. But don't expect me to give you a handout.'

Alissa gaped at the man before her. So powerful, so arrogant, so unfeeling. How could he look her in the eye and refuse her request? How could anyone be so inhuman?

He'd known about Donna's need for cash all this time! She could barely believe it. Her mind reeled at the thought. Yet Dario's calm face revealed a horrible truth: he'd known and he hadn't cared. Any decent man in his position wouldn't wait to be asked, he'd offer to help straight away.

Something inside withered at this appalling revelation about the man she'd almost convinced herself she cared for. She'd thought he was different. Thought she'd somehow been wrong about him. What a pathetic fool she'd been, letting herself fall prey to his powerful allure. She should have learned her lesson about heartless men years ago.

'It's not a handout! It's only what I'm entitled to. What I'm due to inherit.'

'After we've lived as man and wife for six months.'

Alissa jammed her fists on her hips and glared at him, impotent fury igniting. 'You're something else, Dario Parisi. You're a callous, selfish bastard.' Pain tore at her, clogging her throat so the words emerged thickly.

She'd been a naïve innocent. Despite the harsh realities of life with her grandfather she had little experience of dealing with men and none of dealing with anyone like Dario. She'd let his surface charm, those glimpses of a warmer, caring man, lull her into believing she'd somehow been mistaken in her initial estimate of him.

Under the spell of his potent sexual allure she'd forgotten the one thing that counted above all else—his hatred of her family.

So what if he was pleasant and polite to the elderly people at tonight's reception? If his staff liked him? That he had a soft spot for children? Maria and Anna were his people, living on his estate.

Alissa was an outsider. Worse, she was a Mangano, member of a family he abhorred. She knew first-hand about the tight-knit bonds of Sicilian families and their feuds. How could she have forgotten when it was obviously part of what made Dario tick?

She caught her breath on a stifled sob. She'd been ready to believe the best of him too because, despite his fury the day he rescued her, he hadn't resorted to violence as an outlet for his anger. How pathetic could she get?

Her first assessment of him had been right. He was a callous manipulator, more interested in property and ownership than people. Only tonight he'd been accused of causing the death of a rival.

'How do you sleep at night?' she whispered, anguish choking her.

Glittering eyes stared at her from a face pared to stark lines. 'This really matters so much?'

'Of course it matters!' What sort of unnatural sister did he think her?

'You'd do whatever is necessary to help her?'

A tide of hope rose. He was human after all. He'd find a way to help them. He *had* to.

'Of course.'

His lips curled in a dangerous smile. It sent a discordant jangle of premonition through her. 'Then I have a solution to your sister's problem.'

Relief surged and Alissa realised her hands were clamped together so tightly they were numb. Carefully she unknotted her fingers and wiped her clammy palms on her skirt. Dario followed the movement and a *frisson* of unease shivered through her. His gaze was like a hot caress, as real as the touch of a hand.

'Thank you.'

'You haven't heard my solution.'

'As long as there *is* a solution.' Her voice shook.

'Oh, there is.' Her nape prickled at his tone, a soft, predatory growl. 'It occurs to me we're not fulfilling the terms of your grandfather's will.'

'What do you mean?' One moment they were talking about Donna and now the will. 'We're married, living together.'

'But not as husband and wife.'

Alissa's pulse slowed to a dull thud as she looked up into a face devoid of expression, but for the hint of satisfaction that curled the corners of his mouth.

'We're living under the same roof—'

'But not as husband and wife.'

His words sank into her bemused brain. At last she understood that masculine smirk. She froze.

'You want sex!' Her voice was strident with shock.

'Don't sound so surprised. It's what husbands and wives do.'

'But not us! We're not—'

'Married? Ah, but we are, *cara*.' His eyes glittered and that devilish smile widened. 'Here's my proposition. Live with me as a proper wife, in every sense, for the rest of our six months and I'll advance half your share of the money now. The rest you get at the end of our marriage. I need a guarantee you'll stay.'

Alissa opened her mouth to object. No sound emerged.

'I'll see my lawyers and organise the transfer of funds tomorrow...' his voice was a rumble of sensual anticipation '...if you start by satisfying me right now.'

'You're out of your head!' Shock and outrage glued Alissa to the spot. 'You don't even like me.'

Slowly he shook his head, his ice-bright eyes never leaving hers. 'Don't pretend to be so innocent, *cara*.' He stroked her cheek in a caress that detonated explosions of exquisite sensation. 'What's between us has nothing to do with liking.'

He crowded closer and the air between them sizzled. 'I don't have to *like* you to bed you,' he murmured, his voice dropping to a deep suede caress. 'In fact, I'm beginning to think mutual dislike might add a little extra piquancy.'

'You're sick!' she spat back. Yet it was all she could do not to lean closer, to narrow the tiny gap between them till their bodies touched. She turned her head to avoid his hand but he simply wrapped his fingers around the nape of her neck. Tendrils of fire slid through her veins.

'No, not sick. Just a man.' His gaze dropped to her breasts that seemed to swell and tighten under that heavy-lidded look. 'With a man's desires.'

Bemused, she stared into the face that had haunted her dreams. A face so beautiful yet bereft of tenderness. Bereft of everything except unvarnished, unapologetic lust.

Alissa wrenched herself away and strode across the room. Her chest heaved and her legs shook as she forced herself to stop and stare out at the long sweep of the bay, striving for calm. The silver-grey moonlight was chill and stark, like Dario's eyes as he spoke of bedding her.

Her stomach squeezed against the roil of emotions. Disbelief, fear, worry over her sister. And...anticipation.

No! She couldn't want Dario. She wrapped her arms round herself, trying to think clearly. It didn't matter that he'd somehow inveigled his way beneath her defences these last few weeks. Surely she had more self-respect.

'Is this how you get your kicks, Signor Parisi? Playing games with innocent women?' She swung round to face him. Even from half a room away, the intensity of his stare turned her knees to jelly.

'Innocent? The woman who deliberately connived to stop me retrieving what's rightfully mine?' He crossed his arms over his chest in a movement that emphasised the latent power in his big frame. 'The woman whose supposed innocence led her to parties where sex as well as money was traded for designer drugs?'

'I never—'

'Enough!' For the first time Dario raised his voice in a roar that silenced her instinctive protest. It echoed the thunderous beat of her pulse. His eyes meshed with hers, holding her immobile. 'One more denial,' he continued, his voice a lethally quiet whisper, 'and I withdraw the offer.'

'But…'

At the sight of his narrowing eyes and raised brows, Alissa's words petered out. He was utterly implacable. Her stomach dived and her throat closed in a spasm of horror. The dull, metallic taste of fear seared her tongue. The truth didn't matter, not now.

Frantically her mind whirred, but she found no way out. 'You really are as bad as they say, aren't you?' A shudder rippled down her spine as she faced him. 'Cold, clinical, calculating. Completely without remorse.'

Only the knot between his brows hinted at his displeasure. 'I see my fame precedes me. But your views on my character are of no importance.'

Alissa shook her head. Had she hoped even now he'd deny it? 'You're some piece of work, Dario Parisi. I thought I knew

all there was to know about unscrupulous men, but you're something else.'

Dario frowned as if finally her words had punctured his
self-absorption.

Despair wrapped around Alissa's heart. There was no uncer-
tainty in his eyes. Just hunger.

It hurt to draw breath. She reached for the back of a nearby
sofa, needing its support as the world crashed into splinters
around her. Her hand was a stiff claw sinking into the plush
upholstery.

She thought she'd known powerlessness and humiliation. The
night her grandfather had knocked her off balance and down the
staircase when she'd refused to marry Dario. The night she'd had
her fingerprints taken by the police.

But this…

This was the ultimate insult. The ultimate power play.

Grimly Alissa pushed herself straight, angling her chin higher.
She wouldn't give Dario the satisfaction of seeing her pain. Instead
she'd remember Donna's voice on the phone tonight, her brave
attempt to hide her worry and despair. That would keep her strong.

'If I agreed…' She curled her fingers into her palm till the
nails scored her skin and she found the nerve to continue. 'If I
sleep with you, you'll pay half my share of the inheritance
straight away with no arguments?'

His smile was grim, as if her words both pleased and angered
him. 'You'll do more than sleep with me. I want satisfaction. I
want to come deep inside you.' His voice dropped to a pitch that
resonated in her very bones. 'I'll have you, whenever I want,
however I want, until we divorce.'

A cold trickle of despair slid down her back as his words fell
between them. And yet…in the pit of her belly a tiny swirl of
something hot and urgent coiled into life at the idea of Dario,
deep inside her.

Dumbfounded, Alissa stared, not seeing his harsh, gorgeous

face, but instead the pair of them tangled on his bed. It shamed her that a small, wayward part of her found the idea exciting.

She was losing her grip. She'd never been with a man. Never found the courage or the desire to trust a man so intimately with her body, her private self. Yet here, now, his words attracted as well as repelled. She fought self-loathing as well as desperate anxiety.

'No bondage. Nothing rough.' She winced as the words erupted from her mouth. They sounded like capitulation.

'I don't get my kicks that way.' He looked haughty.

'Some men do.' Her voice was uneven but firm.

'You have my word as a Parisi; there will be nothing like that. There are plenty of other ways we can find pleasure together.'

Alissa almost laughed at his certainty. His belief she'd find pleasure with him. She ignored the tiny, traitorous pulse beating at the juncture of her thighs.

'And if I...agree, you'll give me the money tomorrow?' She couldn't believe she was saying this.

'I promise.' He inclined his head.

It would almost be a pleasure to teach him one woman at least wouldn't succumb to his magic touch. She swung round to face the window. By the time she saw the coast by daylight she'd have given herself to Dario.

Panic and disbelief petrified her. Her jaw ached and she realised she'd clenched her teeth so hard her head began to pound.

Could she do it? Her hands twisted as she groped for an alternative. *Anything* to avoid Dario's cold-blooded proposition. But she'd been over her options so many times. There *was* no alternative.

Donna needed treatment sooner than they'd expected. This was the only way to get it. Her options had narrowed to this. Letting him...

Her shoulders slumped as she realised there was no other way. She couldn't even refuse on the grounds that he wouldn't keep his promise. Everything she'd learned about Dario indicated that, though he was merciless, he had enough pride never to break his promise.

Which left her no escape. No alternative but to give herself to him.

CHAPTER NINE

DARIO stood, rigid with anticipation, watching her.

What had got into him? Promising money for sex? He'd never stooped so low in his life.

Something had snapped as he listened to her try to gull him out of his money, appealing to his sympathy. He'd expected something of the sort, but when it came to the crunch, nothing had prepared him for the tidal wave of wrath and disappointment that washed over him when she lived down to his expectations. That she should use her own family as an excuse to get money! That, above all, rankled.

His self-control had shattered under the lethal combination of fury and frustrated desire.

He grimaced at the thought of his lawyers drawing up the contract. Yet not even burgeoning shame at his tactics doused the flare of expectancy as he waited for her answer. The keen blade of desire that ripped through his soul, his conscience, his belief in himself as an honourable man.

His first assessment of her had been right. Strange he felt no vindication at the knowledge. In this one thing he'd rather have been wrong.

His hands bunched in his pockets as she stood staring at the moonlit bay. Suspense gripped him in a vice.

Despite her protests, he'd read her responses. Her gaze

followed him when she thought he wasn't looking, her lips parted a fraction in unwitting invitation when he got close. This would be a mutual pleasure.

As long as she agreed. He scowled as still she kept her back turned. Anxiety juddered through his muscles. This show of reluctance wasn't amusing.

She turned and he held his breath, trying to read her face. Her eyes avoided his. Not a promising start. Dario was stunned to discover he was nervous.

'All right.' Her voice was tight. 'I'll do it.'

Instantly his face relaxed, as if her words eased his tension. That was impossible—it would imply he'd worried she wouldn't agree. Yet this was a game to him, an exercise in domination. He didn't care for her. The knowledge chilled her to the marrow. She'd never be warm again.

'Good.' His lips curled into a slow, sultry smile that, despite everything, made her insides turn over and her heart patter. Was she going mad to react so?

'Come here, *cara*.' His voice was a stroke of velvet, barely concealing an immutable will.

'Now?' She couldn't prevent the catch in her voice as fear overcame desperate bravado. Her fingers clutched frantically at the back of the sofa.

'Now.' He held out one hand.

Looking into the steely depths of his stare, Alissa read an intent that panicked her.

'Not here!'

'Here. Now.' He gestured imperiously, commanding her presence.

He couldn't be serious! She flicked a horrified glance at the door. 'Anyone could come in.'

'My staff have retired for the night. Besides, no one enters this room without my express permission.' He paused and Alissa swallowed as she read the predatory hunger in his face. She'd never felt so small, so vulnerable.

'Unless you wish to back out of our arrangement.' His face tightened, making him look more austerely remote than ever. And more compelling.

He meant it. Absolutely, unequivocally.

That was all it took for cold, hard fury to fill her.

Damn Dario Parisi and his unholy bargain, his superior air and his demands for satisfaction. She'd give him satisfaction all right. Somehow, despite her inexperience she'd manage and in the process she'd show him how much she despised him. Then when she had his money, when Donna was on her way to the US, she'd...

'Alissa.' It was a breath of air, a whisper of sensuous promise. A command.

Gleaming eyes held hers and awareness pulsed between them. She ignored it, delving into the well of indignation that lent her strength to stalk across the room.

Dario barely had time to register satisfaction at her capitulation. Suddenly there she was, soft curves pressing close, her evocative lily scent drugging his senses. Thought atrophied as his libido roared into top gear and every drop of blood rushed south.

She snagged his silk bow-tie in one hand, tugged it undone then ripped it off. The action sucked his breath from his lungs in startled delight. His body tightened predictably as her hands moved to his shirt.

Buttons followed. She was like a dynamo, a whirlwind. He read savage intensity in her small, set face. Not once did she raise her eyes to his. Yet the feel of her neat hands yanking his jacket from his shoulders, reefing his shirt free, aroused him more than he'd thought possible. Only a supreme effort of will held him still, letting her have her way instead of reciprocating. Soon...

She ripped his shirt open and pushed it from his shoulders. Her hands, warm and erotically supple, paused. Her palms slid down, following the swell of muscles. There was a sharp intake of breath and she snatched her hands away as if singed.

It didn't surprise him. He was burning up. Never had he stood passive as a lover stripped him ruthlessly, almost desperately. It was profoundly arousing. His desire was a voracious hunger, an explosive force.

Dario reached out, unable to wait to claim her. It didn't matter what she'd done or why she'd agreed. All that mattered was that she was his. This was more than revenge, more even than desire. This was raw and elemental.

The velvet at her waist was exquisitely soft, but not as soft as her skin. He clamped his hands round her tiny form and dragged her up till she was plastered against his bare chest. She felt like the promise of paradise.

She'd feel better naked.

He smiled as he bent to claim her mouth. That lush, siren's mouth he'd dreamt of so often.

'No!' She wrenched her face from his hold.

She was refusing him! In that instant he felt he'd implode, so all-consuming was his craving.

Then she planted an open-mouthed kiss on his collar-bone and he quaked. Her hands slid down his chest, scraping his nipples and dragging out a groan of longing. Fire shot to his belly. He was so hard, just at the touch of her lips and hands on his bare flesh. He teetered on the verge of losing control.

He fumbled to drag up the skirt of her dress. Velvet bunched in his fingers then slipped as her hands went to his trousers. Lightning shot through him. At the touch of her fingers on his belt his belly contracted. His lungs were on fire, each breath scouring his chest.

He'd expected their union to be spectacular but he hadn't been ready for this cataclysm of sensation. It was exquisite torture as she slipped his belt undone, her fingers provocatively hesitant as she reached for the fastening of his trousers.

Her face was obscured as she kept her head down, watching her hands at work. Finally the fabric fell and he sucked in a thankful breath. He lifted his hands to tug her hair undone but she was too fast. Before he could touch her she was kneeling, undoing his shoelaces.

Potent, erotic images filled his brain as he watched her slide off his shoes, socks, trousers. Images of her pleasuring him with her luscious mouth, her delicate, nimble fingers. He choked back a growl of need, feeling his body race into overdrive.

She'd bewitched him. That was the only explanation. The longer she knelt, head bowed, the harder it was to wrest his mind to any sort of cogent thought. When he had mastery of himself again he'd resent the power she wielded over him. For now he intended to enjoy it.

He grasped her shoulders and pulled her up. His eyes closed as he cupped her neat, rounded bottom and pulled her close. His pelvic thrust against her feminine softness was urgent, instinctive. Bliss.

'Let your hair down.' It was a hoarse plea that emerged as a growled command. He couldn't manage it. It was all he could do to hold himself still. He wanted this to last more than the twenty seconds it would take to rip her underwear off and thrust inside her.

The drumming beat of his need was the only sound as she reached up and dragged out hairpins. Seconds later her hair, long tresses of fire, coiled around her shoulders and further, to rest like a silken invitation across her breasts. How would it look against her pale bare skin? He had to find out.

Drawing on every scintilla of strength he'd once taken for granted, he stepped back half a pace. He shuddered at the loss of body contact. But soon…

He reached for her zip, reefed it down in one desperate jerk, then gathered her skirts in his fists and lifted the dress over her head. His breath ceased as velvet spilled to the floor. He lowered his hands, drinking her in.

She was perfect. Skin like moonlight. So pale and luminous he was almost scared to touch her with his big hands. Her breasts were high and full, her waist a bare hand span, her hips a swell of invitation. Her hair fell in glorious waves around her breasts.

She looked like a mermaid, a Venus, an angel.

Women came to him in silks and diaphanous laces. In sexy bustiers and suspender belts. Alissa wore unadorned cotton. In a deep indigo, it was the perfect foil for her milky skin. And on her legs, lace-topped stay-up stockings. The sight of silky white thighs above sexy dark hosiery was so erotic. She had spectacular legs. She was spectacular everywhere. Satisfaction thrummed in his blood.

'Look at me, Alissa.' Slowly she raised her head. Her lips were firm, rosy curves. Her chin tilted regally, baring her slender neck. Her eyes blazed azure fire.

It took a lust-hazed moment to realise it wasn't the burn of desire. That the angle of her jaw was a challenge, not an invitation. That her lips were primmed, not pouting.

Disbelief tugged at his consciousness. Something like guilt burned acid in his gut. No, not guilt, he assured himself quickly. Alissa was here by choice. She wanted what he had to offer. He wasn't taking advantage of her.

And yet…

And yet everything revolted at the idea of her deigning to pleasure him. This connection between them was mutual. From the first he'd known it. Even now, despite her air of icy self-possession, she couldn't conceal the rapid pulse at the base of her throat, nor her uneven breathing. She felt it too, though she tried to hide it.

And she was going to admit it.

'On the sofa.' The words were a rough order. It was a blow to his ego that he'd stood, a shaking, desperate man, putty in her hands, while she'd kept her mental distance.

He stooped to retrieve a condom from his wallet then took off his boxer shorts. The slide of fabric over his groin exacerbated his anger and his determination. He was so aroused one touch from her would send him over the edge.

He turned and stalked to where she sat primly, knees together, hair a glowing curtain concealing her breasts. That was even more exciting than if she'd been spread naked before him.

Dario pulsed with need and saw her eyes widen as she took in the sight of him, completely bare and hungry for her. Did he imagine it or did she shrink back? No matter. Soon she wouldn't shy from his touch, she'd beg for it.

He felt his smile as a taut stretch of muscles when he knelt before her and put the condom within reach.

'What…?' Her voice petered out as he wrapped his hand round her ankle. So slim, so delicate.

He lowered his mouth to her leg as he unbuckled the tiny strap. Silk stockings and even silkier skin that contracted in shivery ripples as he slid his lips along it. Deftly he slipped off her shoe, taking her foot in his hands as he kissed her calf all the way to her knee. She shifted but he held her, massaging with his thumbs as he kissed back down to her ankle.

Her breathing changed, became deeper. The tension in her muscles eased as his massage relaxed her, made her more aware of physical sensation. He smiled against her instep then moved to her other foot. This time as he progressed with hot kisses up her leg he heard her gasp of pleasure, quickly stifled.

Now both shoes were discarded, he allowed himself access to her thighs. With just a little pressure they fell apart before him and he had to take a moment to focus on his plan. Not to seize immediate gratification but to pleasure her till she relinquished the last of her obstinate self-possession.

Yet it was a moot point who got most pleasure as he trailed caresses up her thigh. His heart pounded so loud it was a miracle she couldn't hear it. At the top of her stocking he slipped a finger under the elastic and swiped his tongue along the lace mark, pleased at her tiny jump of reaction. She tasted honey-sweet. Her single mew of pleasure urged him on, upwards, till the scent of feminine musk tingled in his nostrils.

Resisting temptation, he pressed only the lightest of kisses against flesh-warmed cotton, before caressing her other thigh with his lips, tongue and fingers.

Her languorous ease vanished. Her muscles grew taut. Smiling, he moved up again, lingering a moment to tease her through the fabric of her panties, before sliding his mouth up over her belly to her navel and higher.

It was heaven here, enfolded by her smooth thighs, right at her centre. He buried his face in her long hair, revelling in its fine texture and fresh scent. It spilled through his fingers, an erotic caress against palms already sensitised by contact with velvet-soft skin.

But beneath it was treasure. He released her bra and pulled it away, nuzzling those long tresses aside to discover her pink and white flesh.

The ruched peak of her nipple was beneath his tongue then in his mouth as he suckled strongly. A rapier blade of need sliced through him. He was lost in pleasure.

The swell of her other breast enticed him. He tugged at her nipple with thumb and forefinger while he bit down gently on the other one and was rewarded with a shiver of response. Did she know she thrust herself higher into his embrace with each lap of his tongue?

'Do you like that, Alissa?'

Her eyes glittered feverishly as she struggled for breath. Was she ready to admit to this force between them?

'Yes.' It was a sob and it was music to his ears. He'd needed to hear her say it and know this was mutual.

Only after he'd drawn sighs of shuddering pleasure from her did he lift himself higher. Her breasts cushioned his chest as he kissed her hair, her closed eyes. He licked the outline of her ear and nipped its sensitive lobe.

Dario hoped she felt half the excruciating pleasure he did from this druggingly slow lovemaking. His body strained to breaking point as he leashed his urgent lust. Never had it been so difficult to restrain himself.

Finally he felt the slide of small fingers at his waist, his back, his shoulders. Triumph and relief warred as he bent again to do homage at her breasts. Her hands tunnelled through his hair, grabbing him close.

Alissa shifted restlessly under him and he arrowed a hand down, beneath the indigo cotton, now satisfyingly damp to the touch. Unerringly he found her sensitive nub of pleasure, teasing it with light strokes till she rose helplessly against his every touch.

Never had a woman's response been so powerfully erotic. So satisfying. So arousing. She clamped his face to her breast and her body curved up to his in abandon as if all she thought, all she knew was him.

Yes!

Alissa moaned a protest as he dragged himself back, gulping breaths into his air-starved lungs.

She was the most glorious sight, eyes narrowed to gleaming, provocative slits. Her lips were parted and swollen even though he hadn't yet tasted them. Her hair splayed, a wash of copper and rust streaked with gold, across the dark blue upholstery. And her breasts…

'Please.' Even her voice was a throaty invitation.

Reluctantly he pulled back. 'Patience, little one.'

Swiftly he retrieved the foil package, fitting the condom with a speed born of urgency. He tugged down her panties. She shimmied her hips to ease the way and his belly cramped in excitement. Soon…

When he rose again she was naked, a triangle of russet hair hiding her feminine secrets. The scent of her arousal filled his senses. Very soon he'd learn those secrets. Lowering his head, he dragged his tongue over the path his fingers had followed.

She shuddered into desperate life, her legs clamping his head then falling away as if abandoning the effort.

'Please. Dario.' She urged him higher. He caressed her again, exulting in her response as her hips tilted and she shivered all around him.

'Dario!' It was a low, keening sound but he recognised the desperation in her cry. Didn't it echo his own need?

He rose, about to tell her to stretch full length on the settee so he could blanket her with his body. But even that would take too long. He needed her now.

Instead he clamped her hips and dragged her to the very edge of the seat. He leaned in, hard against her softness, full and ready against her openness.

Lightly he tilted his hips and she rose to meet him. The slide of her slick flesh against him was almost too much. His eyelids flickered as lightning sparked behind them. No, too soon.

With a smile that must have been more grimace, he slid a hand between them, circling, probing, entering. Her eyes widened and heat flared in their blue depths. Again he stroked and she lifted to meet him, her gaze clinging.

How he wanted…no, how he *needed* her.

Her face revealed wonder, as if she'd never known such pleasure. An illusion, of course, but a heady one. He was at breaking point when she reached for him.

'Dario. Now…please.'

His heart gave a huge surge that sent his pulse out of kilter. He dragged her hand up to cup his face and turned to nuzzle it. The scent of Alissa, sweet and salt and absolute temptation, filled him. He licked her palm and her eyes closed.

'Watch me,' he whispered.

She opened her eyes as he lifted her legs round his hips and positioned himself at the entrance to paradise.

'Yes.' It was a hiss of sensual need.

Slowly, inexorably, he surged forward. His shoulders, his

buttocks and thighs, every inch of him strained with tension as he entered that tight, slick space.

Such was the force of will needed to restrain himself he almost missed the tiny sensation of resistance and the breathless grimace that contorted her features.

'Alissa?' Did she hear him? For a moment that looked like distress on her face. He paused, shocked at the message his brain sent him, unable to comprehend it. Then she lifted her hips and thought fled as he slid forward.

Instinct took over as he withdrew then pushed again, more strongly this time. She moaned in pleasure and tension spiralled. He stroked her face, her breasts, encouraged her to stretch up so they were flush together, skin against skin. Heat against heat as he filled her and she welcomed him home with tiny answering movements.

She linked her hands round his neck as she stared into his eyes. His heart swelled to bursting point. A second later, with the first rapid spasm of her body round his, he felt the spark flare in his blood. She cried out as if in surprise and her body clenched around his.

He knew a moment's satisfaction at her climax before he plunged into a vortex of fire. It racked him with pleasure, sent flame racing along his veins. Light exploded in his numbing brain and filled him with ecstasy.

It seemed forever before he slumped forward, pulling her close. His chest heaved as he buried his face against her but the instinct to hug her to him was so strong he didn't care whether he breathed freely or not.

He was too spent to think, to do anything other than ride the aftershocks of cataclysmic orgasm and stroke her hair with fingers that shook.

He'd just had the most fulfilling sexual encounter of his life. With his wife.

A wife who had been a virgin until five minutes ago.

CHAPTER TEN

ALISSA woke to a feeling of wellbeing pervading even her bones. She sensed daylight, yet her limbs were weighted, her body relaxed and replete, her mind empty of everything but the recognition of comfort.

Dimly she realised this was different from other mornings. There was no tension, no anxiety gnawing her vitals the instant she woke to a new day.

Luxuriously she stretched, wondering what—

She froze. The pillow she'd nuzzled was a cushion of living muscle dusted with masculine hair. Her shin had slid between two solid male thighs and one hand was clamped around the curve of a very solid shoulder.

Dario! She was sprawled across Dario like some…

'Morning, *cara*.' His voice, gravel and satin, evoked delicious memories of pleasure. 'I trust you slept well?'

He stroked her spine, making her shiver and arch her back so her breasts pushed into his torso. The friction of skin on skin brought her fully awake. She recognised the pulse of arousal quickening her blood, beating in that tender place between her legs.

She sucked in her breath, drawing with it the rich, addictive scent of Dario's skin. Her bones melted as her body, conditioned after just one night to pleasure at his touch, softened in anticipation.

'I—'

He swallowed her words in an open-mouthed kiss, lifting her up so she stretched full-length against him. As his tongue stroked hers the taste of bitter chocolate and honey, of Dario, filled her mouth. He kissed with the leisurely expertise of a master.

Last night he'd turned the tables, seducing her so thoroughly her angry energy had transformed into erotic abandon.

He'd been so gentle as he wiped away the tears of release and wonder from her eyes. He'd tucked her close and carried her to his suite. Relying only on the moonlight, he'd bathed her with warm water and gentle hands before depositing her, dazed and exhausted, in his bed. He'd spooned close, wrapping himself round her like a blanket. In the night she'd woken to his coaxing voice and it had seemed natural to turn to him. Allow him access to her body. Allow herself the ecstasy of his lovemaking.

He cupped her face and kissed her, his skin with its morning roughness gently abrasive. The stroke of his tongue, the caress of his mouth, the slide of one restless thigh between hers awoke delicious sensations. She craved again the mindless ecstasy, the tenderness, the feeling of warmth that excluded all cares.

'*Cara.*' His voice dropped to a low note that made her shake with desire. It was enough to make her forget…make her forget…

Donna! The blinding flash of remembrance blasted her. She jerked in his embrace as realisation hit.

How could she have forgotten, even for an instant? Her sister was counting on her. Alissa had only gone through with this because… The skein of thought frayed as he tugged her close and deepened their kiss.

Had she submitted to Dario simply for Donna's sake? Or had that been an excuse? A voice in her head accused her of hiding behind Donna's problems so she could reach out for what she'd secretly wanted from the first.

Had she been motivated by altruism or selfishness? And now Dario's ruthlessness, bargaining with her sister's life, came crashing into her brain.

Suddenly her night of unexpected joy was a tainted, guilty pleasure.

'No.' Breathless, she pushed against his shoulders, levering herself away, till she could look down at him.

That was a mistake. His dark hair was rumpled from her touch, his eyes slumberous, sizzling with the concentration he gave to physical pleasure. His jaw was shadowed, giving him a potently sexy bad-boy look. His lips... Alissa looked at that perfectly sculpted mouth, remembering the bliss of his kisses.

'Stop!' Her voice was uneven and her chest heaved against his. She squeezed her eyes shut, torn between self-disgust and delight at the erotic sensation of her nipples against his powerful chest.

'What is it, *cara*?' Dario relaxed his hold and she shuffled away, dragging the sheet across her chest.

Her head bowed as guilt speared her. How could she have forgotten her sole reason for being here? It didn't matter that last night had been the most wondrous experience of her life. What a few moments ago had seemed a short, blissful respite from care now condemned her as heartless and selfish. And condemned Dario as...she didn't want to think about it.

Alissa sat up, focusing on the clock beside the bed. She didn't trust herself to look into the silvery depths of his eyes.

'You promised to transfer the money this morning.' She drew in a sustaining breath. 'The banks are open now.'

Dario couldn't believe his ears. He reared back as if she'd struck him.

Minutes ticked by as he stared at Alissa. The woman who'd given him more passion, warmth and pleasure than he'd ever had. Who'd made him question everything he'd been so sure of yesterday. Not with clever words, but with the apparent honesty and generosity of her body's responses. He'd actually believed she couldn't be the mercenary little go-getter he'd thought her. He'd decided that, despite all the evidence, he'd somehow been mistaken.

His mouth tightened as he fought down rising bile. His bed reeked with the musky scent of sex. Of her deviousness and his gullibility.

When he'd discovered her to be a virgin he'd felt guilt at pressuring her into his bed. He'd felt like the lowest slime ball that had ever slunk out of a gutter. Until his senses overrode his conscience. After that he hadn't been able to stop himself, for the ecstasy surpassed everything he'd known.

Afterwards he'd believed his view of her character flawed. She couldn't be all he'd thought her. Yet his guilt hadn't stopped him reaching for her again. His scruples were no match for his need.

He'd told himself that this morning, in the clear light of day, he'd discover the truth.

But the truth was, despite her virginity, she'd played him all along. There'd been no connection between them, no melding of souls that went beyond the boundaries of physical pleasure. He'd imagined that as he'd reeled from the most erotic, satisfying experience of his life.

Shame flooded him that he'd let himself imagine there was anything more between them. She'd laugh if she knew.

'I said the banks are open now.' Her chin jutted up, her mouth settling in a firm line.

His hands clenched as he surveyed her. She looked like a queen refusing to acknowledge a dirty peasant, despite the fact they were in bed together.

Was she trying to put him in his place? After last night's intimacies?

Ingrained memories of condescending looks and arrogant words rose instantly. For years he'd endured the stigma of not fitting in, not being good enough. He'd been too independent to please prospective foster parents. They'd wanted him to forget his past and his family and pretend to be theirs. When he hadn't he'd been labelled difficult, a kid who'd never amount to anything.

He thought he'd obliterated any sensitivity to such things. He *had* done. Until Alissa played havoc with his libido and his judgement. Until she'd awakened emotions long forgotten. *That* was what he couldn't forgive.

'Probably not the best way to greet your lover,' he drawled, trying not to react to the seductive picture she made, her hair a sensuous curtain around pale, perfect shoulders. The sunlight outlined her sweet curves through the linen.

'Why not?' Her voice was sharp. So different from last night's throaty purrs and moans of delight. He wished he could have her now as she'd been then. Pliant, eager and so responsive. 'It's the only reason we're in bed.'

Fury surged, stirring an unfamiliar turmoil of emotions. How could he be disappointed that she was motivated by money? That last night had been about hot sex and mercenary gain?

'You'll need to improve your bedside manner, *cara*, or your next lover mightn't be so generous.'

'Generous?' It was a squawk of outrage. 'You've got a hide.' Her eyes flashed fire that scorched his bare skin. 'There's nothing generous about you, Dario. You'd sell your grandmother if you thought you could turn a profit.'

A shaft of anger pierced him at her accusation. She couldn't know how much family meant to him.

'I earned every penny of the money you owe me.' He watched her swallow hard. Her eyes flicked away as if the sight of him offended her sensibilities. 'No doubt you'll make sure you get your money's worth over the next months.'

A chill descended with her words. Part of him cringed at the truth of what she said. Even now, nothing would keep him from taking her to his bed again and again. Despite his lacerated pride, one night with her wasn't enough. The realisation made him lash out.

'Then it's as well you have a natural talent for pleasure, isn't it, Alissa?'

Satisfaction was an inner glow as he watched a blush rise in her throat. Surely at least some of her responses had been genuine. He recalled her wide-eyed wonder as he'd brought her to the brink of climax again and again. The sweet pulse of need in her body, the clumsy yet entrancing way she'd taken her turn at pleasuring him.

Hell! He was hard just remembering.

'Why were you a virgin?' He'd blurted the words without thinking, still shocked by the discovery.

Her brows arched. Energy sizzled between them at the intensity of her glare.

'Because I don't like men,' she snarled.

Stunned, he registered a plunging sensation in the pit of his belly. She couldn't be… No, not when she'd responded to him the way she had.

'At least not enough to want to go to bed with one of them,' she added, as if reading his thoughts.

'Why not?' He had to know.

'I've yet to have a close relationship with one who doesn't want to control my life.' Her eyes flashed. 'Can we cut the chat while you organise my money?' Her words might have been chipped from glacial ice. Just like her profile of regal disdain.

Deliberately Dario stretched and linked his hands beneath his head. He'd promised so he'd deliver on the money. But it went against the grain to jump to her tune.

'Congratulations,' he murmured. 'You have to be the most blatantly greedy woman I've met.'

'You expect me to apologise?' She leaned forward as if spurred by feelings so strong she couldn't sit still. 'You think I should be ashamed, when you *know* why I need it?' To his astonishment tears glittered on her lashes before she blinked them away.

They were back to that. Suddenly he'd had enough of this conversation, sickened by the way, even now, she tried to play on his sympathy. He flung back the sheet and stalked to the dressing room to tug on some jeans.

'Don't think you can walk out on our deal.' She'd followed him. He swung round to find her, swathed in a trailing sheet, hair in disarray and a mutinous expression on her face. The hunger for her grew in him anew.

What did that say for his judgement? He turned his back so she wouldn't see how she affected him.

A small, firm hand arrested his movements, dragging at his arm, trying to tug him around.

'You *owe* me, Dario!'

He swung back, face taut as he battled the urge to silence her with his mouth. Disgust filled him at the predictability of his need for this woman.

'Enough! Get me your bank details. By lunchtime you'll have enough cash to keep a dozen farms afloat.' Or, more likely, spend it on herself.

'Farms? What farms?' She frowned as if he spoke a foreign language.

Had she forgotten the excuse she'd used last night? The need to save her sister's cattle station? He shook off her hand, zipping his jeans and reaching for a T-shirt. 'You said you want cash for your sister.'

'That's right.' She stood behind him. He felt her warmth, smelled her skin. 'But she's not buying a farm.'

'Saving a farm, then.' He flung out one hand in a dismissive gesture. 'Wasn't that your excuse for wanting to cut a new deal? To save her from foreclosure?'

Silence. Except for a hissed intake of breath.

'You thought that's why I wanted the money?' Something about the quality of her voice made him still. He turned to find her white-faced. 'You said you'd had us investigated, that you knew all about us.'

He nodded. 'I paid an Australian detective agency. They were thorough,' he said, thinking of the dirt they'd dug up on her past.

'Not thorough enough,' she murmured. 'They didn't check

medical records, did they?' He watched her press one clenched hand to her breast.

'Not that I know of.' There hadn't seemed a need. 'Why?'

Alissa lifted her chin to meet him stare for stare. 'Because my sister is ill. Her only hope is a radical new treatment in the US. Without it she'll die.' She breathed deep. 'It costs a fortune. Money Donna and her husband don't have. Money I could only get by marrying you.'

The world tilted and spun crazily off its axis as he met her unwavering gaze.

It couldn't be. And yet…it would be easy enough to check. She must know that.

Dario's lungs laboured. His chest constricted under the impact of an invisible blow that shoved him back against one mirrored wall, leaving him stunned.

Could the investigators have missed something so crucial? He'd employed the best. But perhaps the best hadn't been enough. He should have used his personal staff.

He met her unflinching gaze, read the shock in her face, the horror in her eyes. His certainty cracked.

It was possible.

A yawning chasm ripped open inside him as the implications struck home.

Che diavolo ha fatto? What the devil had he done?

'Tell me.' His voice was strained and his features set in a mask that hid his emotions. Only his searing eyes hinted he felt anything at her news.

Alissa told herself she didn't care what he thought. All she cared about was saving Donna. If she concentrated on that she could ignore the crazy yearning for the comfort of his strong arms about her. Tremors of fatigue and reaction ran through her and she slumped into a chair.

'Tell me.' The words were stronger now. He planted his feet

wide. He'd dropped the T-shirt and stood bare-chested, his hair all dark, tousled locks, his arms at his sides.

She couldn't stop a thrill of appreciation at his male perfection. She hated herself for it.

'There's nothing to tell.' She lowered her gaze. Even his feet, strong and sinewy, reminded her of how she'd abandoned care and duty and given herself to pleasure in his embrace. Self-disgust was bitter as aloes in her mouth. 'The specialists in Australia can't help and our health system won't fund her treatment overseas.' She fisted her hands in the cotton at her breast.

'When did this happen?'

'We got the news a couple of months ago.'

Alissa saw emotion flicker in his eyes. Did he believe now that she'd only gone through with a marriage for Donna's sake? That, after refusing to marry him when her grandfather was alive and then again immediately after the old man's death, this was why she'd agreed? She bit her lip. She shouldn't care what he believed.

'You didn't ask me for money then.'

'Ask you?' Fury surged. 'Why would you help? From the first you made it clear you hated me because of my grandfather's plans for us to marry.' She sucked in oxygen, trying to calm her racing pulse as she remembered the contempt in Dario's eyes, the mocking chill in his tone. 'I had everything planned with Jason until you stormed in breathing fire and brimstone and wrecked everything.'

'You could have told me.' His voice was low.

'As if that was likely!' She fixed him with a glare. 'You gave the impression you'd revel in our misfortunes.'

'You believed I'd ignore the fact that your sister was dying?' His jaw hardened. 'That I'd stoop so low?'

'What? Lower than forcing me into bed when we hate each other?' Her voice broke and she looked away, wrapping her arms tight round her torso. She lashed out at Dario but it was she who felt guilty. She who'd let herself wallow in pleasure when she should have withstood his seduction. She who'd forgotten her responsibility to her sister.

'You thought I'd let her die. That I would negotiate such a bargain knowing all the circumstances.' His voice held a strangely distant note that made her turn.

What she saw made her suck in a stunned breath. A stranger looked back, eyes devoid of life, lines etched deep around his mouth. An unnatural pallor greyed his skin.

'Dario?' Shock held her rigid. He looked as if he'd been dealt a fatal blow, sheer willpower keeping him on his feet. She'd been so ready to believe the absolute worst of him last night. It seemed now she'd been wrong.

Regret streaked through her. Could she have convinced him of the truth last night? He'd been implacable. But then she'd been so ready to judge him badly. She'd let her prejudices blind her. She'd judged him her grandfather's equal, reviving old fears and mistrust.

She opened her mouth to speak when he forestalled her.

'What's wrong with your sister? Was it an accident?'

'No, nothing like that. Donna has liver damage and other complications. It's a result of…problems. She went off the rails for a while.'

'Define "off the rails".' His gaze narrowed.

Alissa stared at one mirrored wall, seeing Dario, tall and imposing, and herself, huddled in a swathe of white.

'Drink. Guys. Drugs.' After a lifetime of obedience to their grandfather, Donna, the quiet one, had finally rebelled in spectacular fashion. Alissa hadn't been able to stop her. Familiar guilt scorched her conscience. It was as if Donna had sought the quickest way to destroy herself: sex and drugs at seventeen, rehab at eighteen. Married and dying at barely twenty.

A deathly chill ran up Alissa's spine.

'She was under age at the time. Yes?'

Alissa turned to find Dario watching her, something like understanding in his eyes. 'How did you know?'

'The investigator got some of it right.'

'I worked two jobs, making ends meet after we left home. Donna was old enough to live with me, but not old enough for clubbing.' But that hadn't stopped her. 'I didn't realise she'd used my ID to get into nightclubs and bars until it was too late.'

'That explains it. She was mistaken for you. Her behaviour, the drugs, the men…it was her, using your ID, pretending to be you.' His expression was grim as he held her gaze till she assented.

'And the night of the drug bust?'

Alissa couldn't look away. That invisible connection she'd imagined last night was back, drawing her into his power. 'I went looking for her.'

'Did she have drugs?'

Alissa nodded. She'd been desperate to get Donna out, away from the guy with the sweaty, possessive hands who was all over her kid sister, away from the poison she'd been putting in her body. Even now, if Alissa shut her eyes, she could imagine the throb of mind-numbing music, smell the rank scent of crowded bodies, see Donna…

'You took the drugs from her when the police raided, didn't you?'

'What else could I do? She's my little sister!' For a moment longer she met his piercing grey eyes then turned away. 'It was best in the long run. The shock of my arrest convinced Donna to get help. She's been clean ever since.'

Much good that would do now she's dying.

Alissa's lip wobbled and she bit down fiercely, refusing to give in to fear. They'd find a way. Donna would get her treatment. She'd survive.

'Alissa.' His voice tugged her back from her thoughts. 'I'm sorry. Sorry for everything. I—'

'No!' She leapt to her feet, staring into a face etched in slashing, spare lines that might even signify pain. Into eyes shadowed with regret. 'I don't want to hear any apologies. Not now.'

Her emotions were too raw, too confused for her to cope with any more. She ached with disappointment and fury. Against them both: him for discovering her carnal, selfish weakness and her for giving in to it, despite the dictates of self-respect and duty.

'All I want is the money I earned last night.'

CHAPTER ELEVEN

'YOU look much better now, sweetheart.' Alissa smiled into the wan features so like her own and gave thanks. Even now, so soon after her treatment, Donna was much improved. It was everything Alissa had hoped and prayed for.

'Don't exaggerate.' Donna smiled weakly from her hospital bed. 'I've seen the mirror.'

'I know what I see, and it's all good. David is as smitten now as he was four months ago when you married. He thinks you're the most beautiful girl in the world.'

Donna's eyes softened at the mention of her husband, just as his did whenever she was around.

It must be wonderful to share that kind of love. A squiggle of emotion stirred inside Alissa, the same sensation she felt whenever she saw her sister and brother-in-law so blatantly in love. It wasn't jealousy. She didn't begrudge them their happiness. Yet Alissa couldn't help wishing she too could experience that sort of devotion.

Inevitably her mind turned to Dario, the silent, distant, ultra-efficient man who'd arranged Donna's treatment. He'd seen to it she jumped to the top of the specialist's patient list. He'd organised everything, including a nearby apartment for David and a manager for the property in their absence. He'd hired a luxurious house for himself and Alissa a short walk from the hospital.

Donna and David thought those were the actions of a besotted husband. Only Alissa knew they were the result of a guilty conscience.

Dario would never look at her with wonder in his eyes. He didn't want a long-term lover, at least not one like her. His tastes ran to tall brunettes, not short, sassy redheads. Their night together had been an aberration. He hadn't touched her since. One night was all it had taken to cure him of his desire. Pain scoured her at the thought.

'Just like the way Dario looks at you,' Donna said.

Alissa dredged up a smile, playing along with the fiction. 'Dario has too much control to wear his heart on his sleeve.'

'That's what you think. You don't see how he looks at you when you're not watching.' Donna shook her finger knowingly. 'His eyes go all hot and hungry. Honestly, it makes me burn up just seeing it. Especially since he's such a hunk. No wonder you couldn't resist him.'

Alissa stared at her sister, her automatic denial disintegrating on her tongue. How she longed for that to be true. Even knowing Donna was exaggerating, Alissa felt her heart give a fillip of excitement.

Much as she tried to despise her husband for the unholy bargain he'd forced on her, she couldn't deny her attraction to him. It was as strong as ever.

Stronger. For now she knew the ecstasy to be found in his embrace. The tender way he treated a lover, as if she was the only woman in the world.

The fact that he was driven now by remorse, so attentive to her needs, to her sister and her husband, revealed him as a man trying to atone. There'd been no mistaking his shock when he'd learned about Donna.

'You should spend more time with him, instead of spending your days with me.'

'Why do you think I'm in the States?' Alissa smiled, thinking how great it was to have Donna well enough to fantasise about her older sister's non-existent love life. 'It's for *you*, sweetie.' She brushed a lock of hair from Donna's face. The maternal gesture was completely natural. Alissa had been looking after her since their mum died.

'But you could fit in a second honeymoon with your gorgeous husband.' Donna waggled her eyebrows.

Alissa forced a laugh past her choked throat. Weeks ago, when she'd confronted Dario after their night of passion, she'd thought she'd never want to be intimate with him again. Now the knowledge that he slept in the massive suite next to hers tortured her with guilty longing. She wished he'd return to Sicily instead of working here with two secretaries and a barrage of phones.

Surely if he wasn't here she wouldn't feel this edginess? This hunger for his touch?

Was it because she'd never been with another man? She hadn't known how spectacular sex could be. She recalled Dario's taunting voice, telling her she had a talent for pleasure. Heat flared in her cheeks. Could he be right?

Right or not, it was clear she no longer held any appeal for him. He was scrupulously distant and reserved.

'Alissa?'

'Sorry. I was miles away.'

'But not happy thoughts. Don't you want a second honeymoon?'

Did she? Alissa bit her lip, realising she did. Despite his managing ways and their disastrous relationship to date, she wanted Dario. Desperately.

It was desire but it was more too. An unbreakable connection. When he entered a room she shivered, hoping and fearing he'd take her in his arms. The comfort she'd found in his embrace was magical, though she told herself she should despise him. She even missed their verbal sparring!

He was her guilty secret.

'Alissa? What's wrong?' Donna's voice was sharp. 'It's about the marriage, isn't it? I *knew* there was something you weren't telling me.'

Alissa met her sister's penetrating stare and silently cursed. Donna was far too acute sometimes.

'Why should there be anything wrong? As you say, I've married a gorgeous hunk who swept me off my feet,'

'Except you're not the sort to be swept off your feet. You always had guys trying to catch your interest, but you ignored them. Men have never been your weakness, not like me.' She hung her head.

'Don't!' Alissa squeezed her hand. This wasn't the moment to revisit the past, when rebellion had led Donna into promiscuity with the worst sort of guys. 'That's over. You have David now.'

'I have, haven't I?' Her quick smile faded. 'But what about Dario? Your romance was so sudden. And I always thought you wanted to live alone after Granddad.' She paused. 'Dario just burst onto the scene around the time you said you'd find a way to…' Her words ended in a gasp.

'You're imagining problems where there are none,' Alissa began. 'Dario and I—'

'He's the one, isn't he? The one Granddad wanted you to marry? The mega-rich Sicilian!' Horror dawned in Donna's voice. Tenaciously she gripped Alissa's hand. 'Tell me you didn't marry him for my sake. For the money.'

'Of course not. I…' Under Donna's stare, she heard her words peter out. Alissa had never lied to her sister. Except about this. 'We just…'

The door to the private room swung open and Donna's doctor, flanked by a phalanx of junior medicos, entered.

'Mrs Kincaid. I'm glad you're awake. I have the results of your tests.'

Dario strode to his bedroom. He'd worked past midnight again, hoping to dull the emotions swirling inside him and upsetting his equilibrium. Guilt and regret as well as desire. The un-abashed hunger for the woman he'd manipulated and, in his ar-rogance, abused.

For the first time ever he was ashamed of his actions. Yet even shame couldn't blunt the keen edge of his need. She despised him. Hell! He despised himself. Yet he craved her. Her spirit, her strength, her firebrand attitude, the way she stood up to him and refused to be dominated.

The way she gave herself so unstintingly to physical passion. *The way she made him feel.*

He worked nineteen-, twenty-hour days, trying to exorcise her from his mind. Yet it was fruitless. For the first time, rebuilding the Parisi fortune and prestige held no allure.

He didn't understand how she fired this craving in the blood. Despite her guts and beauty, she was nothing like the woman he'd planned to take as his life partner.

His footsteps slowed as he passed her room. He hadn't seen her this evening. She'd stayed late at the hospital and he'd kept to his office.

He paused. That was when he heard muffled weeping. Instantly he tensed. Through everything she'd never cried. Except when he took her virginity. He'd convinced himself then that she'd wept in ecstasy.

This sounded like despair. His gut twisted. What could make his courageous wife cry as though her heart had broken?

He shoved open the door and stepped inside. She was hunched on the window seat, arms wrapped round her knees. Her feet were bare, her hair a tangled swathe of coppery red burning like fire in the lamplight. She wore a shapeless sleep shirt that was down-right ugly with its inane cartoon characters printed on pale cotton.

She looked perfect.

His insides clenched at the sight of her. Desire, need and something more. Something…warm and protective.

'Alissa.' In an instant he crossed the room, hands in pockets to prevent himself reaching out. She'd feel contaminated by his touch. Helplessly he watched her shake as a tremor racked her. 'What is it? Speak to me.'

Hearing Dario's voice, Alissa gulped down the salty knot of emotion filling her throat and scrubbed her hand across her eyes. She hadn't seen him for days and now he had to find her like this.

'Alissa! Tell me what's wrong.' His voice was rough, that gravel-over-satin tone she'd last heard in his bed. Something unravelled inside and her breathing snared like a bird in a hunter's net.

'Nothing's wrong. I'm fine.'

'It doesn't look like nothing.' Long fingers clasped her chin and turned her face up. Tendrils of forbidden delight wove out from his touch. She was so susceptible.

She scowled. Had she interrupted his sleep? But a glance showed he wore dark trousers and a white shirt. Her gaze dropped from his intense expression to the V of golden skin at his collar-bone. She breathed deep but only succeeded in filling her lungs with his scent.

An instant later he hunkered beside her, his heat enfolding her as he wrapped his arm round her back.

'Is it your sister? Is it bad news?'

Alissa shook her head, feeling more foolish than ever. 'N-no. She's all right. The doctor came with the f-final test results.' Desperately she tried to master her voice. 'It will take her a long time to recuperate but the treatment was a success.' Her lips pulled tight in a trembling smile. 'She's going to live.'

A large palm circled slowly between her shoulder blades. 'Then what's the matter?' He was so close Alissa could feel the puff of his warm breath on her cheek. She bit her lip. 'Alissa?'

'I d-don't know!' It was a wail of despair. She should be ecstatic. She *was* ecstatic. This was the best news. What was wrong with her that she couldn't just rejoice?

She'd shared a celebratory dinner in the hospital with Donna and David then made her excuses, knowing they needed time alone. She'd been fine as she entered the elegant house Dario had hired with its discreet smell of money and its plush, indifferent silence. Her smile had waned on the way up the magnificent empty staircase. By the time she'd soaked in the travertine spa there'd been a curious ache in her chest. Then something had cracked inside and she'd collapsed, bawling her eyes out.

'I never cry,' she sobbed. 'Never.'

'Shh. I know. I know.' His arm tightened and she burrowed closer.

She felt as if a dam had split, smashing under the force of a welter of emotions. Through everything she'd been tough, never giving up hope. She'd been strong for Donna even in the darkest hours, first with their grandfather, then during Donna's addiction and illness. She'd fought Dario's demands too, every step of the way.

But now…Alissa had lost the strength that had sustained her for so long. She was confused and afraid.

Strong arms drew her up against a hard chest.

'What are you doing?'

'Putting you to bed. You can't stay there all night.'

Alissa didn't mean to snuggle against him. He was the enemy, the man who'd put her through hell and somehow bewitched her soul. Yet she couldn't resist leaning into him as he scooped her up. She wanted to revel in the illusion that she was protected and cared for. Cherished.

Minutes later she lay huddled at the centre of her too big bed. Shivers racked her until he slid in behind her and pulled the covers up.

'No. Don't!' She tensed and scrabbled to escape. 'I don't want—'

'Shh, Alissa, I'm going to hold you. Nothing more.' He wrapped his arms round her and pulled her against the furnace-like heat of his bare chest. Caution told her not to let down her guard but something deep inside urged her to trust him.

Her need for comfort was too strong. She slumped against him, grateful beyond words that he was here. She didn't understand what was happening. Never had she experienced this loss of control. She sniffed back the despised tears and turned her head into the pillow.

'You're overwrought. You need to get warm.'

Overwrought! She'd never had the luxury of giving in to nerves. She was the strong one, the protector, even sometimes the scapegoat, putting herself between Donna and the old man when his temper grew dangerous.

'What's wrong with your arm? Have you hurt yourself?' She looked down to find she'd been rubbing her forearm. It was a nervous gesture she hardly noticed now.

'It's an old injury. It doesn't hurt any more.'

'What happened?' His words feathered her ear and a sliver of heat pierced her, warming her from the inside.

Alissa stared across the room, stunned to be sharing a bed with Dario, soaking up his warmth and reassured by his presence. It was insane, but it was real. It felt so good.

'Alissa?'

What did it matter? There was no point in secrets now.

'I broke my arm a few years ago when my grandfather knocked me off balance and I fell down a flight of stairs.'

The sudden spasm of Dario's arms around her midriff robbed her of breath.

'*Dio buono!* You could have been killed.'

'I was lucky.' She watched his hand curl round her wrist, stroking as if to soothe the long-dead pain. The sight of him touching her, the sensation of his caress, unknotted some of her coiled tension.

'How did it happen?'

'One good, hard push.' Her lips twisted on the memory.

'It was deliberate?' His voice was a husky croak of disbelief.

'With my grandfather it was always deliberate.' There was a

sense of release at sharing the truth. Residual anger against the old man was enough to banish her teary weakness, for now at least. 'He made my mother's life hell when she brought us to his home after our father deserted us. When she died the old man turned his attention to me and Donna. *Necessary chastisement* he called it.' The bitter taste of memories coloured her words.

Dario's iron-hard arm around her waist tightened even as his touch on her arm gentled. Alissa suppressed a sigh as that simple, tender caress eased her bone-deep tension. He had such power to heal as well as to hurt.

'No one saw?'

She snorted in disgust. 'No one wanted to see. I tried to get help when I was young, when I was worried for Donna. But it was easier to turn a blind eye, especially as my grandfather was an important man. He had money, power and reputation. No one wanted to know. He ensured the town believed I was ungrateful and unruly, causing trouble.'

Alissa drew a shaky breath. 'He was obsessed with controlling our lives, from who we met to how we dressed. The worst wasn't the beatings but the mind games, the manipulation, the continual battle for dominance. If he'd had his way we'd never have made a decision for ourselves.'

Each word plunged into Dario's brain like a stiletto blade. His meeting with Gianfranco Mangano had confirmed the old man was the sort of snake with whom he'd never normally do business. Only Dario's vow to his long-dead parents, his vow to retrieve what they hadn't been able to, had made him swallow his pride and deal with such a man.

He remembered the glitter in Mangano's eyes as he'd complained of his granddaughter's wild ways and her need to learn obedience. The vengeful twist to his mouth had been ugly as he'd declared his intention to marry her to a 'strong man' who'd keep her out of trouble.

146   BLACKMAILED BRIDE, INNOCENT WIFE

At the time Dario had believed the unscrupulous old swindler had simply reaped what he'd sown in the form of a granddaughter as appalling as he.

Dario slid his fingers over the soft skin of Alissa's inner arm, amazed at the strength of this tiny woman. His stomach clenched at the history of abuse she'd revealed.

Wrath, white-hot and untrammelled, fired his blood. Animals like Mangano didn't deserve the blessing of a family. Especially not when others, loving and responsible, were denied the chance to grow old with their children.

Alissa felt so small and defenceless cocooned in his arms. He hated the thought of her hurting. Of her fighting such battles with no one to protect her.

Ice clamped his chest as he recalled the stark anxiety in her eyes when he'd confronted her in the boathouse. His fear for her had made him lash out and she'd withdrawn, dragging herself to her feet. Had she thought he'd strike her?

Dario's heart hammered as guilt scored him.

'What made him hit you?' The thought of her, crumpled at the foot of the staircase in Mangano's ostentatious mansion, made him ill.

'I stood up to him,' she murmured in a voice so low he barely heard. 'A friend had a party and for once I was determined to go. It was a 60s retro night, everyone wore miniskirts or flares. But it wasn't wild. Her brother even drove me home.' She paused and he felt her draw in a deep breath. 'I'd hoped to slip in quietly but my grandfather was up late because you'd visited unexpectedly.'

Memory blasted Dario. Of how he'd sat in his car outside the Mangano house, seething at the old man's insistence on marriage to his granddaughter. Dario had seen her, bare legs and long, loose hair, smiling at the guy who'd driven her home. Even in the gloom she'd been breath-stoppingly gorgeous. He'd been jealous as hell of the youth, just because he'd been on the receiving end of her megawatt smile. The memory had infuriated him ever since because of its unfailing ability to stir his libido.

'So, it was punishment for being out without permission. But you weren't a child.' There'd been no mistaking her for anything but a full-grown woman.

'I lived there till Donna was old enough to go too. I couldn't leave her with him.' Alissa shifted as if to move away and he firmed his hold till she subsided against him. Did she have any idea what it did to him when she wriggled like that? Her perfectly rounded bottom was pure invitation against his groin. His boxers were no barrier to desire. Jagged darts of heat speared him as he fought not to react.

It took a moment for her next words to penetrate his rapidly fogging brain. 'He was angry about the party. But what really did it was our argument about you.'

'Me?' He shook his head, trying to clear it of subversively potent images of Alissa inciting him to take her. 'You argued about me?'

She nodded and her hair slid against his bare chest, a silken caress that loosened all the power in his limbs.

'He demanded I marry you. He'd talked about it before but I don't think he believed it was a real possibility until you visited.' The uninflected way she spoke chilled Dario to the marrow. He sensed the pain it hid.

'He was so excited, so determined that I obey. He wanted it arranged as soon as possible.' The chill became a hoar frost of tension.

'What happened?'

'We argued. He demanded I sign a marriage contract and I refused.' Alissa paused long enough for Dario to count the blood pulse three, four, five times in his ears. 'The old man lost his temper and lashed out. I went to hospital with a broken arm and a cracked rib.'

Her words, so matter-of-fact, revealed a horror he'd never guessed at. He felt contaminated, dirty, realising he'd unwittingly been culpable in injuring her. If he'd continued to refuse Mangano's scheme as he had originally, this wouldn't have happened.

'I can't breathe,' she gasped and Dario discovered he was squeezing her in a vice-like grip. Instantly he loosened his hold, his body trembling with the force of a fury that had no outlet.

'I'm sorry, Alissa,' he whispered against her velvet-soft cheek. 'So sorry.'

How much damage had he done to this woman?

No wonder she avoided him. Understanding hollowed his chest. He could barely imagine the stress she'd been under. Only now, with the easing of fears for Donna, had Alissa's defences weakened. Her formidable control had shattered.

What a burden she'd carried. And for so long. Trying to protect her sister against their monstrous grandfather, and against Donna's foray into drug abuse.

Then he, Dario, had come on the scene. Another man with money and power. Another man determined to bend her to his will. Determined to believe the worst.

His gut twisted as he realised how he'd compounded her pain, how he'd compounded her fear of being manipulated and abused by a man.

At least he hadn't beaten her as her grandfather had.

No. Instead he'd forced her, a virgin, to give herself for his pleasure. Self-contempt was a scorching brand burning his innards as he remembered her shock and defiance that night.

By all that was right he should release her instantly.

But he couldn't relinquish his hold.

Guilt, shame, regret, even his well-honed sense of honour was powerless against the force of his desire—his selfish need for the woman who despised him.

He cradled her close, arms tightening possessively.

He couldn't let her go. Not yet.

CHAPTER TWELVE

ALISSA'S eyes felt puffy when she woke. The salt tang of tears was still on her tongue.

How long since she'd cried? Years. Soon after her mother died Alissa had learned that, perversely, her grandfather enjoyed her fear and pain. She'd bottled up her emotions and pretended to be stronger than she was.

Until tonight when her worst fear had miraculously been removed and she didn't need to be strong any more.

Weeping had left her numb and empty. No, not empty. There was effervescence in her blood, a tingle of relief. Donna was safe! The words rang over and over in her brain.

After the heavy, dreamless sleep she felt warm and weightless as if she floated on a tropical sea.

Yet it wasn't the ocean that cradled her. It was the sinew and flesh and hard muscle of a man. In her sleep she'd snuggled closer to Dario till she lay across him, breast to breast, one foot tucked between his bare knees, one hand in the softness of his luxuriant hair. She threaded her fingers deeper into his locks, overwhelmed by the sense of rightness here in his arms, her lips against the steady pulse at the base of his throat.

Her heart turned over as she remembered how he'd held her, simply held her when she needed comfort. His soothing words, his gentle caress. As if the stranger with the harsh, judgemental expression had never existed and there was only the man who'd made such surprisingly sweet love to her in Sicily. Who'd rescued her from the sea. Who'd organised Donna's life-saving treatment.

As if, despite what had gone before, he was the one man she could rely on. The one man she could trust.

Which was the real Dario?

His circling thumb at the small of her back made her breath catch. Whorls of pleasure erupted from the spot, twisting with devastating accuracy to all the erogenous zones he'd discovered that night in Sicily. Her lips parted in a gasp that brought the tang of male flesh to her mouth.

In an instant comfort transformed into desire.

All it had taken was one tiny, almost innocent caress.

Last night's storm of emotion had left her defences shattered. She couldn't even pretend to indifference. She arched into him like a cat stretching to a caress.

This was right, she knew it in her bones. Logic would call her a fool, but now, bereft of every barrier she'd used to keep the world at bay, this craving wouldn't be denied. *For Dario.* For the ecstasy he'd brought to her untutored body. For the potent sense of connection they'd shared, as if, for a few moments, their twin souls joined.

It was irresponsible but she didn't care. Not now when everything in her confirmed he was the one, this was the time. No matter how short-lived the moment.

She pressed her lips against his neck and slicked her tongue along his hot, salty skin. She almost purred aloud at the taste of him in her mouth.

The thumb at her back was replaced by a hand slipping down, squeezing her bottom till she pressed against him. There she found the rigid proof of his answering need. He felt so *good.* Restlessly she circled her pelvis. Instantly his hand clamped her motionless against him.

'You're barely awake, Alissa.' His voice was a harsh rumble vibrating in his neck, against her open mouth. 'You'd better stop.'

Why? In case she changed her mind? Hardly, not when need thrummed through her like a life force.

Or was it that he didn't want her? He hadn't wanted her in weeks. Yet there was no mistaking his desire. She rotated her hips again and was rewarded by a surge of power, bringing his erection hard against her. His fingers tightened on her buttock.

'Alissa.' It was a warning growl. The timbre of his voice, low and rough, stirred her senses. He was so very, very male. For only the second time in her life, that knowledge was a potent aphrodisiac.

This might be her only chance to experience again those wonderful sensations. Through all the worry over Donna and outrage at Dario's actions, nothing had suppressed her yearning for his lovemaking.

Life had taught her that happiness was rare. She determined to seize what she wanted now.

Raising her other hand, she bracketed his skull with her fingers and pulled herself up to plant a kiss on his mouth. His next words were muffled as she slipped her tongue between his lips and kissed him as he'd taught her.

Instantly desire became marrow-deep need. He was big and warm and luscious. She cupped his jaw. The texture of his roughened skin against her sensitive palms sent a jolt of fire to her womb. He tasted…perfect, like dark, bitter chocolate, rich and strong.

Alissa shifted, straddling him as she stretched high. She delved deeper, tongue stroking, till finally, with a rippling shudder of reaction that vibrated through them both, Dario came alive. His tongue tangled with hers, his head angled to access her mouth better. His hand slipped under the stretchy cotton of her nightshirt to mould bare buttocks with long fingers.

His other hand tugged down those silky boxer shorts and Alissa gasped as his erection rose under her. She squirmed and his hand tightened, holding her still as he deepened their kiss.

Now his other hand covered her breast through the cotton, stroking, squeezing, then flicking across her nipple.

She groaned and gave herself up to the assault of pleasure. Energy roared through her, spiking with each caress of his hands and mouth. Yet she was filled with a weighted laxness that made her putty in his hands.

It wasn't enough. She needed him. With a supreme effort she managed to co-ordinate her fingers enough to fasten on her nightshirt and drag it up. He grabbed the hem from her and ripped it over her head.

Alissa wanted to look down at him then. To see the desire in his crystal-grey eyes, to see his hunger for her.

Yet...would his need match hers? Or would it be tainted with pity? Pity he'd felt as she'd told him about her past and her grandfather's abuse. Pity for the desperation she couldn't conceal. He wanted her, but surely not with the soul-deep yearning she felt.

Coward that she was, she kept her eyes shut, telling herself it was only physical release she sought. Knowing it for a lie, but unable to face him. Not yet.

'Alissa.' The hoarse whisper, the light touch of his fingers at her breasts, almost cracked her resolve. She wanted again that connection, as if they shared their very souls, watching each other as they gave themselves.

But this was enough. It had to be.

With a whimper of pleasure she pressed close, absorbing his sultry heat, kissing him desperately. He matched her lips to lips, tongue to tongue, breath for breath. Her lungs were ready to burst, her blood pounding a desperate rhythm, when he lifted her up away from him. She made to protest but stopped as she felt the blunt, velvety nub of his arousal. She moved back and was rewarded by the feel of him sliding, long and powerful, against her.

'Dario.' It was a choked gasp, part plea, part wonder.

Strong hands steadied her, holding her safe as her legs

trembled. She planted her hands on his shoulders, gripping tight as the tremor became a shudder of anticipation that shook her whole frame.

'Come to me, Alissa.' His voice was a throaty purr. 'Come to me now.' He urged her higher. Willingly she rose, felt him there, where she most needed him, then let his gentle guiding pressure bring her to meet him.

Her lips parted in a gasp of ecstasy as they joined. Even the first time he hadn't filled her so completely. His power and sensuality stole her breath.

He moved and a cry of delight broke from her. Dario clasped her hips, urging her to move. Lights blazed behind her closed lids and spasms of greedy pleasure rippled through her.

'Please, Dario.' Her fingers curled into his flesh but he didn't stop. His movements grew stronger, sharper, coiling the tension to breaking point till with a single smooth thrust he flung her into ecstasy.

Rivers of molten delight filled her, starbursts of sensation as she pulsed in his arms, completely lost to all the world but him. He surged up, higher than she'd thought possible, and flooded her with his warmth. The instant of mutual pleasure grew and expanded as they shared ecstasy.

Finally, shaking, he drew her down, wrapped his arms round her and held her against his juddering heart.

His lips moved against her hair, nuzzling her ear and a belated blast of sensation burst through her. She stiffened then collapsed, boneless.

Dario scooped her close, astounded by the perfection of what they'd shared. Sex had never been this good. Something about this woman was different—beyond his experience.

Alissa had turned to him. Even after what he'd done to her, taken her virginity to satisfy his lust, misjudged her in the most appalling way. That she should invite him so boldly was a wonder. He'd been hard-pressed to hold back long enough to give her pleasure in return.

Was it just stress, the need for comfort, that prompted her to seduce him? Or desire, strong as his own?

He remembered how she'd kept her eyes shut, as if she couldn't bear to look at him, even as he pleasured her. Regret was a slow-turning stab of pain low in his belly.

Had she simply used him for the physical release he could provide? He couldn't blame her if she had.

Yet he wanted more than a frantic coupling in the dark. He wanted her again, and, he realised with a certainty that stunned him, he wanted more than her body.

He wanted all of her.

This was utterly new territory. It defied every certainty he'd constructed for his life and he had no idea where it would lead.

Alissa shifted and his body stirred. That ripple of awareness so soon after satiation was unprecedented. But everything about her was different from previous experience.

This possessiveness was a new phenomenon. He'd never shared his lovers but nor had he felt such a primal sense of ownership. Was it because she'd come to him a virgin? He slid his hands over her curves, hauling her close.

The knowledge he was her first, that all she knew of physical intimacy she'd learned from him, fired his blood. He felt like a conqueror who'd won the best prize.

He wanted… His hand paused in its proprietorial sweep over her hip and thigh. Unseeing, he stared into the cool light of dawn as he realised what they'd just done.

Unprotected sex.

It was unthinkable. Unbelievable. He'd never in his life so lost control that he'd forgotten a condom. Never.

His jaw clenched and his groin tightened as he relived the pleasure of that release, hot and vital with no barrier between them. Pleasure such as he'd never known.

There was no danger of disease, but there was the risk of pregnancy. He waited for the inevitable sense of entrapment to surface.

Alissa sighed and nuzzled his neck. All he felt was satisfaction that he might have planted his seed in her.

What the hell was happening to him?

Three hours later Dario had showered, shaved and dressed while Alissa slept. He should tackle the mountain of work awaiting him, yet he didn't leave. He sat in an armchair and pretended to read a report.

His gaze strayed to the woman curled in the centre of the bed. The curve of her bare shoulder and the spill of long, bright hair fascinated him, drawing his attention from fiscal details. Her face, so beautiful in repose, looked relaxed for the first time in weeks, though smudges of tiredness were visible beneath her eyes.

He watched her wake and stifled rising tension. How would she react? He'd given up all pretence of indifference. Somehow, without him understanding how, she'd become important to him. He needed her. At least till this…fascination wore off, as it eventually would.

'Hello, Dario.' His body responded to the huskiness of her just-awake voice. 'I didn't expect to see you here.'

Typically, she'd tackled the issue of his presence head-on. His lips quirked appreciatively. It wasn't just her body he admired.

'Good morning, Alissa. You slept well?' He saw her cheeks flush. Remembering her high colour as she'd climaxed only a couple of hours ago, he felt his body harden.

'Yes, thanks. About last night…'

He had the impression she chose her words with care. Tension dragged at his sinews, stiffening his muscles. He put the report aside and crossed his ankles, projecting an air of relaxed attention.

'Yes?' He watched her sit up, drawing the sheet over her breasts. The sight of her, tousled, pink-cheeked and naked beneath the fine linen, was disconcertingly provocative. He gripped the arms of the chair tight.

'Thank you,' she murmured, her blush growing rosier as her chin tipped higher. 'I'm grateful.'

Grateful! She was grateful to him for making love to her? Unable to remain seated, he sprang to his feet. Of all the responses he'd imagined, gratitude wasn't one he'd considered. He shoved his hands in his pockets and strode across to stare out the window.

'There's no need for gratitude,' he said through gritted teeth. It had been his pleasure. All pleasure.

He didn't want thanks as if he'd done a trifling favour. He wanted her to need him as he needed her.

'Of course there is.' Her sincerity made him turn. Her eyes blazed and she held his gaze without blinking. 'I want you to know I'll keep my part of the bargain. I'll be your *proper* wife, as we agreed.'

Blue fire flashed in her eyes and he knew what she meant by 'proper' wife. His senses clamoured, knowing he'd have her just as he'd desired these long weeks.

But, searching her face, he discerned no excitement. She looked like a woman talking only business. No sign of passion. The realisation cut the ground from under him. Disappointment welled like blood from torn skin. Yet he wouldn't refuse her offer.

'Thank you, *moglie mia,*' he said, summoning restraint. He had to go before he did something stupid, such as let her see how much he needed her. 'I appreciate your reassurance. And now, forgive me but I have business to attend to.'

Unable to resist, he drew her hand to his lips, pressing an open-mouthed kiss on her palm. There was fierce satisfaction at the sound of her indrawn breath and the sight of her pulse racing at her wrist.

She was as vulnerable to this passion as he.

Yet gratitude had prompted her promise to share his bed. That shredded his pride.

Surely a flame that flared so bright must burn itself out soon. This was a temporary aberration. In time his reaction to her would dull. Then he could find a docile Sicilian wife to bear his children. To restore the Parisi family in fact as well as name—those goals had sustained him for so long.

That was what he wanted, the perfect life with no untidy emotions to trap the unwary.

Unless Alissa was already pregnant.

A thrill of possessive pleasure sideswiped him. Till he realised how slim was the chance she'd conceived.

He forced himself to drop her hand.

He ignored the whisper of conscience that warned he acted out of pride as much as need. That for the first time he desired a woman more than she desired him.

The notion was unsettling.

No, this was a matter of mutual passion. He would make amends for the wrongs he'd done her. He'd care for her as she deserved. And, he vowed, he'd give her more pleasure than she'd ever known until the time came to part.

Alissa stared at the closed door and her heart plummeted. When he'd kissed her hand with barely leashed passion heat had risen again between them. Hope had risen too. Hope that he felt that spark of connection.

But when he'd raised his head and looked at her with eyes like winter he'd doused her hope. Was the magic she'd felt with him one-sided? Had he felt nothing more than physical release? The sort of release he'd had with countless women?

His expression when he'd thrust aside her gratitude had been forbidding. But he'd saved Donna's life and last night he'd offered Alissa the comfort of his embrace, no strings attached. He'd listened, he'd held her close and she'd felt as if nothing could hurt her again. She'd never felt so cared-for in all her life.

Had he no idea how special that was? How incredible and fragile was that tender bud of trust she felt? Apparently not. He'd refused to acknowledge her thanks.

Perhaps her gamble was sheer folly. After all, what did she know of intimacy between a man and a woman? Only what she'd learned with Dario. Maybe what seemed extraordinary to her was nothing of the sort.

Yet her feelings were so strong they couldn't be denied. She'd turned to him this morning wanting comfort and that sense of belonging she'd discovered in his arms. His tender response was everything she'd wished for.

She'd made up her mind to continue their bargain, hoping that by the end of their allotted time she'd discover what these raw new feelings meant. Perhaps even discover that Dario felt them too. Despite his ruthless streak, she knew there was another side to him. A tender, caring, compassionate side.

She remembered how he'd pulsed within her and how, as she realised they'd forgotten a condom, there'd been no panic. Just acceptance and a thrill of pleasure.

Had she taken leave of her senses? *Wanting* to stay with the domineering man who'd disrupted her life?

It was crazy. It was asking for disappointment. Yet Alissa could no more keep her distance from Dario than she could ignore him.

CHAPTER THIRTEEN

IT WAS early evening. The square of the tiny Sicilian village was packed when Dario gave in to the clamorous roar of the crowd and got to his feet.

Alissa watched him on his way to the gaily decorated dais where the mayor had already given a speech. Dario paused here and there at the tables to exchange greetings.

Her husband was the centre of attention. It wasn't simply his superb looks, or the lithe grace of his ultra-fit body that held everyone's gaze; an aura of power crackled around him like static electricity. Beaming faces, wrinkled and smooth, old and young, followed his progress.

Alissa's Italian had improved in the months since their return from the States. She followed the mayor's speech, littered with references to Dario's vision in rejuvenating traditional local industries like olive oil and ceramics production in what had recently been a depressed area. How he'd endowed schools, backed cottage industries and offered work. To these people Dario was a hero. Nor was that new. Whenever she accompanied him to community events she was overwhelmed by the affection in which he was held.

Who was the real Dario Parisi? A civic hero? Absolutely. Plus he had the absolute devotion of his staff. They genuinely respected him.

He'd moved heaven and earth to save her sister and ensure she and David were financially comfortable. He'd been under no obligation to do that, but he had. Because he felt guilty for his actions? Perhaps that was why he grew stiff and formal whenever she attempted to thank him.

He loved children, shedding his formidable reserve whenever Maria and Anna were around, becoming tender, fun, the sort of man who made a woman dream of the future.

How did she reconcile his generosity with the coldly conniving man so obsessed with recovering his family estates? Who had, if the story was true, caused the death of a competitor? That man seemed no longer to exist. She saw few traces of him.

Alissa still didn't understand what motivated him.

Sometimes she felt she was almost close enough to know him. When he made sweet love to her through the night, or just held her in his arms when her period started. He hadn't known how desperately she'd craved his tenderness then. It was crazy, her disappointment when she had learned she wasn't pregnant. She should have been thankful there'd be no baby from their marriage. Yet she'd felt bereft.

Even then he hadn't chosen to sleep elsewhere. As if it wasn't just sex he wanted. As if he too wanted more.

Did he feel that strong link between them?

Some days she was sure he did. Days when, to the amazement of his staff, he took a holiday from his all-consuming work and spent the day with her. They swam, explored local sights, or lay in bed and made love.

Yet whenever it seemed they were on the brink of an understanding, he withdrew. There was a barricade around him that no one breached. Except perhaps Caterina Bruzzone, the old woman who was as close to Dario as family.

Alissa's gaze lingered on Dario, masculine perfection in a dark suit, holding the crowd in the palm of his hand.

The man who, she finally admitted, held her happiness in that broad palm too.

'He is a fine man, Signora Parisi.' A middle-aged stranger leaned close, nodding approvingly. 'We are lucky in your husband's patronage.'

Blindly she smiled and nodded, tears blurring her vision. She was too emotional these days. With the destruction of the defences she'd used to protect herself from her grandfather, and later, the man who'd bought her in marriage, she had no reserves left.

She watched Dario, stepping from the podium to rousing applause. Her heart swelled. With pride? Longing? Love?

She pressed her lips together to prevent a gasp. No, not love. Gratitude for saving Donna. And affection. After all, Dario had introduced her to wondrous physical passion. They said a woman kept a soft spot for her first lover.

She wasn't so foolish as to fall for her husband. That would be disaster. He didn't want love, would be horrified if his convenient wife became sentimentally attached.

'It was a good day when he returned,' the stranger continued. 'We were doomed with old Cipriani in charge.'

Yanked out of her thoughts, Alissa turned and stared.

'Old Cipriani?' Bianca's father? The one driven to suicide. 'What was wrong with him?'

The stranger shrugged. 'Best not to speak ill of the dead.' Then he turned to shake hands with Dario, who'd forged his way back through the throng.

'Are you ready to go now, *tesoro*?' The rare endearment took her by surprise. Dario leaned close, the warmth of his smile encompassing her.

'The celebration's not over.' She struggled to control her racing pulse and look unruffled.

He shrugged, spreading his palms wide in that habitual gesture which once had so annoyed her. Now she enjoyed the wry curl of laughter on his gorgeous mouth. 'The party will go into the night. We can stay if you wish.' He bent nearer. 'Or we could go home and celebrate privately.'

His voice was a husky burr that melted her insides. The knowing look in his eyes and the promise of pleasure sent heat flaring along her cheeks.

Alissa put her hand in his, enjoying the touch of his fingers, firm and familiar. 'Let's go home.'

A gleam darkened his eyes, then his face smoothed into the unreadable mask he wore so often. 'I hoped you'd say that.'

Fifteen minutes later they sped along a winding road with spectacular views of the coast. The Lamborghini's engine growled as Dario manoeuvred the car expertly round a bend.

With his jacket slung across the back seat, his sleeves rolled up and pleasure curving his lips, Dario looked sexier than ever. Almost carefree.

How rare that was. Usually he was busy, driven by business responsibilities and other cares he didn't share with anyone. He was so self-contained.

'What is it?' He didn't take his eyes from the road but he knew she watched him. Just as she could tell when he entered a room by the tingle of awareness at her nape.

She shook her head. 'Nothing.'

Dario swung the car round another curve and they swooped down to the coast. The Castello Parisi loomed on its promontory, a reminder that they'd soon be home.

Home for the next couple of months, Alissa reminded herself with a twist of regret. Not once had Dario hinted he wanted her to stay beyond their six months. Ruthlessly she squashed her hurt.

'More than nothing. You've been watching me since we left. What's on your mind?'

She hesitated, then decided to take the plunge. 'Tell me about Signor Cipriani.'

Dario's hands tightened on the wheel, his shoulders hunched so slightly she might have imagined it. The speedometer flicked to the right as they sped faster.

'What do you want to know?' he said finally as he swung the car off the road into a narrow lane running straight for the sea.

'I've heard things. And I wondered—'

'Whether it's true he killed himself because of me?' There was no inflection in his voice but the carefree aura had disappeared. Regret swamped her as she took in his white-knuckled grip and the taut angle of his chin.

Did she really want to know? Wasn't it more comfortable not knowing?

'No. I…'

'Of course you do.' His voice was flat as he pulled up. He switched off the ignition and the sound of waves invaded the still interior of the car. 'Come. Let's walk.'

It was only when they got out that Alissa realised they were on Dario's private property towards the end of the beach nearest the *castello*.

He held her hand as they picked their way down the path to the beach. His grip was impersonal. Gone was the closeness they'd shared today. Had she imagined that?

She blinked back hot tears. She didn't know where she was with him. She only knew she wasn't ready to leave him.

When they reached the firm-packed sand he let go and stooped to remove his shoes. Silently she followed suit.

'It's true,' he said in a sombre voice as they walked down the beach. 'He died because of me.'

'No!' She grabbed his hand, curling her fingers round his. Instinctively she knew he wasn't to blame. Her heart thudded in distress till finally he returned her grip.

Relief bubbled up. The fact that he'd accepted her touch and he held her tight made something soar inside. Warning bells jangled. She was in so deep. She cared for Dario too much.

'How can you know it wasn't my fault?' His gaze held hers in the gathering darkness.

'I just do.'

There was no sound but the shush of waves as he stared down at her. A breeze played in his hair, but Dario didn't move a muscle. After endless minutes he turned and led the way further down the beach.

'Guido Cipriani had something I wanted—a business started by my family. It was the last asset my parents kept before Mangano, your grandfather, ruined them.'

Dario picked up his pace till they strode. 'He deliberately destroyed them. It took years of bribery and corruption, plus some unfortunate investments and a downturn in the markets. His hatred of us was blood-deep.'

'I know.' She remembered his gloating pleasure in triumphing over the Parisis.

Dario sent her a swift sideways look but kept walking.

'I determined to get the company back. I've made it my life's work to recoup all the assets the Parisis owned.'

Alissa shivered as the square battlements of the *castello* loomed ahead. In the fading light it had a threatening air. She'd bartered her freedom so Dario could obtain that medieval symbol of power and family pride.

'You're cold.' He tugged her close. 'We should go back. The temperature is dropping.'

'No. I'm OK.' She needed to understand this to understand Dario. 'What did you do?'

'I offered to buy but he wouldn't sell. He'd put in decent managers who'd kept it profitable but eventually even they couldn't keep it in the black.'

'Why not, if it was profitable?'

'Cipriani was a gambling addict. He wasn't just siphoning off profits, he stole from the business to pay debts to people who...enforced payment.'

Alissa shivered, imagining who those people were. 'What happened?'

Dario's arm tightened and she leaned into his solid warmth. 'When the time was right I offered again.'

'Bianca said you offered less than its value.'

'Much she'd know,' he said under his breath. 'All Bianca Cipriani knew was the business supported her luxury lifestyle. She's typical of her set. Never had to sully her hands with honest toil. When the cash dried up she looked for someone to blame.'

Dario stared at the *castello* rising above them. 'Cipriani had no choice. It was sell to me or let the authorities uncover his theft.' Dario smoothed a hand back through his hair, a gesture she'd never seen him use. 'He signed the deal then went and shot himself. He couldn't face the loss of honour, no longer able to support his family.'

Dario's profile was grim, flesh pulled taut over bone. The sight of his pain made her chest ache.

'That wasn't your fault.'

'Wasn't it? If I hadn't badgered him to sell, if I hadn't been there ready to jump in—'

'Someone else would have.' She touched his arm. 'Did you lure him into his gambling debts?'

'Of course not.'

'Or use underhand tactics to ruin him?'

Dario drew himself up. 'No! I'm a Parisi, not a...'

Not a Mangano, that was what he'd been going to say.

'If you didn't ruin him, how can you blame yourself?' For Dario did blame himself, it was there in his grim face.

He shook his head. 'I should have seen it coming and prevented it. His wife...'

Alissa heard the tightly controlled emotion in his voice and pressed closer. He wrapped his arms about her and she was surrounded by his spicy scent and heat. His heart pounded near her ear.

'I don't understand. If your funds just covered his debts, where does Bianca get money? She doesn't look short of cash.'

Dario's hand palmed her hair. 'Of course I topped up the sale price to ensure his wife was provided for. Her husband was dead.

She had no one else. It seems she's foolish enough to let Bianca squander it.'

'Of course.' Alissa stifled a shocked giggle. There was no 'of course' about it. Judging by the couture cut of Bianca's outfit and her lavish jewellery, Dario's idea of 'topping up' the sale price had been absurdly generous.

Was there anything more ridiculous, more utterly unfathomable, than this man's code of honour? To blame himself for a death that wasn't his fault, then make amends in the most generous way? He had such an inflated sense of responsibility.

Alissa stood on tiptoe and pressed a kiss to his lips.

'What's that for?' he growled as if taken by surprise.

She shook her head, not ready to examine her reaction. 'Come and sit out of the wind.' Alissa led the way to the sheltered rear of the beach. She had too much on her mind to go back yet.

After a moment he sat beside her, his legs stretched out on the sand, his arms propped behind him.

For a long time they were silent. Finally, encouraged by the gathering dusk and Dario's earlier revelation, she asked the question that had been on her mind so long. This seemed her best chance to understand.

'Dario, why is it so important you get back everything the Parisis owned?'

'It's my birthright, my obligation to my family,' he shot back without pause. 'What man wouldn't wish to restore his family's fortunes?'

'Surely your wealth is more than your family ever owned.' She knew he had controlling interests in ventures right across Europe and North America.

'I promised to restore what was ours,' he said in a tone that made her slip him a sideways glance. His profile was hard and sharp as volcanic glass. 'I won't stop till I've done it. It's a matter of honour. Of duty. The rest is a bonus.' He flicked his fingers as if the millions, or perhaps billions, he owned were a mere bagatelle.

'Promised whom?' His family? Had he really no one of his own? Despite the affection in which he was held locally, he was the most alone person she'd met. Totally, frighteningly self-possessed, except for the rare occasions he let down his guard with her.

The waves rolled in and ebbed back again and again. When he didn't answer, her throat closed.

It didn't matter that he wouldn't confide in her. After all, she wasn't his real wife. She was a temporary bed partner. Resolutely she blinked moisture from her eyes and planted her palms on the sand, ready to rise.

Long fingers encircled her wrist. 'My father. I promised him before he died.' Despite the clipped words, his voice was resonant with deep emotion.

'I'm sorry, Dario. I take it he died before you approached my grandfather about the *castello*?'

Even in the gloom his scrutiny was so intense it was like a touch. 'He didn't tell you?'

'I know nothing about your family except Gianfranco hated them because a Parisi jilted his sister.'

Slowly Dario nodded then turned to watch the waves. His free arm lifted and a pebble arced into the water.

'It happened when I was seven.'

'I'm sorry,' she repeated inadequately.

'My father was determined to recoup his losses. Some of them, like the *castello*, had been in our family for generations. Generations of proud tradition, plus blood, sweat and hard work.' Not by the slightest inflection did he give a hint of emotion. It was as if he recited a rehearsed piece. Yet his bunched muscles and the tendons straining at his neck told another truth. He lobbed another pebble into the water, the movement one of perfect grace and restrained savagery.

Alissa shivered as a chill wind brushed her skin.

'He'd take me on his knee and tell me about family traditions built over centuries. About our history and our obligations to the land and our people.' His lips curved but it wasn't a smile. 'He planned to regain it all. The lost family honour as well as the assets. To rebuild the Parisi name till it commanded the respect it once had.'

Dario's voice held a note that filled her with foreboding. Another stone splashed in the shallows. 'There was an opportunity to start again, a venture in northern Italy. If it worked he'd have enough to return to Sicily and start again.'

'But it didn't happen.' Alissa's heart was in her mouth, anticipating the tragedy she knew must come.

'No.' He drew in a breath so deep his chest expanded mightily. 'There was a storm. The ferry was overcrowded. The authorities said later there should never have been so many people aboard.'

Alissa slipped her fingers from his loosened grip and covered his hand. It fisted, rock-hard in the sand.

'There wasn't enough room in the lifeboats. Papa wouldn't let me stay with him. He said it was my duty to go. He made me promise…'

For the first time she detected a tremor in Dario's deep voice. She leaned in, resting her head on his shoulder, hoping to bring some small comfort. Her heart plunged at the picture his words conjured: father and son ripped apart in the mayhem of a sinking vessel. She should never have asked about this.

'He demanded you carry on his plans if he couldn't?' It made a horrible sort of sense. Dario had been a kid when he'd shouldered this burden. No wonder he was so driven, so implacable in his quest.

'No, I offered that freely. As his son it was my duty to restore the family honour.'

When he spoke of honour she heard an echo of her grandfather and his obsession with righting past wrongs. But now she understood the difference between Dario and the old man. Dario's pride wasn't rooted in hate but in love. Love for his family and a deep-seated sense of duty.

'He made me promise to look after the others.' Dario's voice was so low she barely heard him.

'Others?' His body stilled as if he stopped breathing. Fear clamped her chest.

'My little brother, Rocco, and my mother. It was late in her pregnancy and she wasn't feeling well.'

The words echoed into a silence so profound Alissa couldn't even hear the sea. Only the sound of his words thudding like bullets into her flesh.

'And they…did they…?'

'The lifeboat was overcrowded,' he said once more in a colourless voice that froze her blood. 'It capsized in the rough seas. I held on to Rocco as long as I could. But I couldn't save him.'

'It wasn't your fault.' The words were automatic as she struggled to comprehend the enormity of his loss. How had he coped with such an appalling tragedy?

'I should have been able to save one of them. Just one.' His voice thickened and he drew another mighty breath. 'Their bodies were never recovered.'

Alissa turned blindly and wrapped her arms tight round him as if she'd never let go. It didn't matter that he was big and strong and stoic. She'd heard the pain in his voice. Her heart broke at the thought of that little boy losing everyone who loved him. Believing it was his fault.

How could his father have put that responsibility on him? It wasn't fair. Then she remembered Dario saying he hadn't wanted to leave his father. She'd guess even at seven Dario had seen himself as a man, willing to stay like his father and take his chances on the sinking ferry. Perhaps the promise to care for his mother and brother had been the only way to get him onto the lifeboat.

Her silent tears soaked the fabric of his shirt as she hugged him close. His body was rigid.

'Where did you go…afterwards?' Her words were choked.

'An orphanage on the mainland. I lived there till I was old enough to strike out on my own.'

Alissa sucked in her breath, her mind reeling. Never had she suspected anything like this. She'd assumed Dario had grown up with privilege if not with the money he'd accused her grandfather of stealing. Dario had such an unconscious air of command she'd figured he'd honed it through years of haughty condescension.

Yet he'd grown up alone, without anyone of his own to love. How wrong she'd been.

'And then?' She had to know the rest.

'I returned to Sicily. I began as a labourer but discovered I had a talent for business. After a few years I was working for myself, employing others. I brought Caterina over. She'd been house mother at the orphanage and promised to be my housekeeper when I set up my own home.'

Alissa felt a flash of relief as the grimness of his tone abated a fraction.

No wonder he'd kept the truth of their marriage from Caterina. He hadn't wanted to hurt her, the one person he cared for. He hadn't wanted her to know he'd married in order to wrest back his family's past glory.

And no wonder he hated the Manganos.

'You blame my grandfather.' Her tone was flat.

'If he hadn't swindled my family we'd never have been on that ferry,' he growled with awful simplicity. 'He didn't just steal the *castello* and the money, he stole my family, the life we should have had together. Of course I blame him.'

Now so much made sense. Dario's accusation that she didn't deserve the advantages she'd had at his family's expense. He'd thought her a privileged bimbo like Bianca Cipriani. That she'd had family, wealth and security when he'd had none. Gianfranco had stolen his future, his very family.

Even as she dragged his stiff form close and rose on her knees to cradle his head against her breast, Alissa knew the comfort she offered could only be transient. He might find ease, release, even pleasure, with her. But in his mind her grandfather's sins would always taint her.

These past weeks, despite the warmth and pleasure they'd found together, there'd still been unspoken barriers between them. Now she knew why. Dario would never look at her without remembering.

The hopes she'd secretly cherished splintered like fragile spun glass. There could never be a future for her with Dario.

He pulled her to him and something melted inside.

It was the worst possible time to realise she loved him.

CHAPTER FOURTEEN

'SHE can't come to the phone, Donna. She's still asleep.' A smile tugged Dario's mouth as he thought of Alissa, sated and exhausted after a long night of loving.

Last night he'd bared his soul to her. He didn't understand what had prompted him. But for the first time ever he'd known an overwhelming urge to share himself.

It had felt *right*.

She'd stripped him to the bone, scoured away everything till he'd been exposed and naked, more vulnerable than he'd felt since he was seven and they'd told him he'd lost everyone.

Now he felt renewed, reborn, with a strength and wholeness that made his blood sizzle. Alissa had done that for him.

They'd made love on the beach with a desperate ardour that barely slaked his need. He'd been insatiable, for her touch, her body, and more, that sense of completeness only she gave him.

Back home they'd barely made it to the bedroom before they'd turned to each other. The wild yearning hadn't been his alone. Alissa had matched his passion with a desperation that stole his breath.

Finally their frantic need had been assuaged and he'd lain with her in his arms, marvelling at the incredible sense of contentment filling his parched soul.

Alissa was…special. She was…

'Pardon?' His musing ceased abruptly as he took in his sister-in-law's words. 'What did you say?'

'I said Alissa can come to us when she moves back to Australia. Now we're financially secure, thanks to you, she can holiday here before returning to Melbourne.'

Dario's brows furrowed. He spoke slowly, as if one wrong syllable might shatter something vital. 'What makes you think she's returning to Australia?'

'It's all right, Dario. You don't need to pretend. Alissa explained the arrangement: six months then you go your separate ways. It won't be long till the time's up. I know she's looking forward to picking up her old life…'

Donna's words faded to a background buzz as his mind whirred into top gear. Alissa had told her sister *that*? Had talked about relocating as soon as possible?

Searing pain banded his torso, a fiery loop tightening till finally he remembered to breathe. His heart hammered against his ribs, pounding out a desperate protest.

From the jumble of his emotions he identified the one that hollowed his bones.

Fear.

He was terrified by the idea of Alissa leaving. Of losing her.

Dario put out an arm and caught the corner of his desk. Winded, disbelieving, he stared at the contracts stacked for his signature. He felt a powerful urge to swipe them off the table and into oblivion.

How insignificant they seemed in the face of this brutal revelation. Suddenly the world shifted into focus, revealing a truth he'd never suspected.

The momentary weakness passed and he straightened, sure of himself again. He was used to snap decisions and trusting his instinct. He was used to taking charge.

He had no doubts about his course of action.

'Things have changed, Donna. Alissa won't be going to Australia except on visits. We're staying married. Permanently.'

* * *

Alissa stopped in the doorway of the study and clawed at the doorjamb for support. She couldn't believe her ears... Dario soothing her sister with lies about them staying together. Dario saying that their marriage was permanent.

Ecstatic hope burgeoned, only to be dashed by common sense. Whatever Dario's motive it wasn't that he loved her. Love wasn't on Dario's agenda. She'd discovered that last night when he'd torn out her heart with his story. The only love he felt was for the memory of his family. His only need his obsessive quest to restore the past. She ached for him and for herself, because she realised now it was impossible for them to stay together.

Last night she'd loved him with a desperation born of knowing this must be the end of their intimacy. She'd promised to stay six months. But she couldn't destroy herself by giving herself again to him, fuelling her love when he'd never return her feelings.

Anguish scooped out the place where her heart had been. In his mind she'd always bear the stain of her grandfather's role in his family's ruin.

She had to save herself while she had the strength.

Quietly she stepped inside and snicked the door shut, determined to face him before her resolve wavered.

Alissa marvelled at his arrogance as he spun Donna more lies. Anger sparked and she welcomed it. Anything was preferable to the helpless yearning that had tormented her since she'd woken in his empty bed.

She crossed her arms over her chest and waited. He ended the call and turned to stare out the windows, his gaze fixed on the *castello*. Why wasn't she surprised? It was all he really cared for. Old stones and dreams of past glory. Not the love of a real flesh-and-blood woman. He yearned for the past, for what he'd lost. And who could blame him?

The knowledge pumped her blood faster. Her mouth twisted.

She was jealous of a pile of rocks and mortar! The disturbing re-alisation lent her the strength she needed.

'What do you think you're doing, lying to my sister?'

He spun round and Alissa had the momentary satisfaction of seeing shock stark on his handsome face. Then the shutters came down. He looked as warm and approachable as a marble statue.

His aloofness stiffened her resolve. She could cope with that. It was the hidden Dario, real, vulnerable and hurting, who shat-tered her barriers with his tenderness and passion.

'Come in, Alissa, and sit down. We need to talk.'

'We sure do,' she muttered as she paced across the room. 'You've got a nerve, feeding her that story.' Yet even as she lashed her anger her weaker self longed for him to pull her close and say it was true: he wanted them to remain man and wife because he loved her.

She wanted it so badly she trembled.

'Here.' He gestured abruptly to the long lounge.

The place where they'd first been intimate. Piercing bitter-sweet memories surfaced.

'No, thank you.' She halted before his desk, keeping a safe distance between them.

Eyes the colour of winter rain meshed with hers. The danger-ous undertow of desire tugged at her. She looked away. 'Tell me,' she demanded.

'Your sister's call pre-empted a discussion I'd planned to have with you.' He sounded relaxed, as if he were discussing anything but their future. 'I've been considering our marriage…'

'And?' Her heart hammered in her throat.

'All things considered, it seems logical to make our arrange-ment permanent.'

All things considered… Suddenly Alissa wished she'd taken his offer of a seat. Her legs were rubbery, her knees quaked. She braced her palms on his desk and breathed deep. 'All what things?'

He took a stride towards her then halted, jamming his hands deep in his pockets.

'We got off to a rocky start.' He ignored her stare of disbelief. 'But we've settled into a good relationship. You like the life here. Sicily suits you.' His gaze snared hers again and she read approval in their glittering depths. Heat corkscrewed in her stomach.

'You've fitted in perfectly, coping with society events and local gatherings like the one yesterday. Fitting in with *me*. With my lifestyle. We're good together.' She waited, breathless for him to say the one thing that mattered, the one thing she needed to hear.

He remained silent and something cracked inside her.

Alissa licked her lips and discovered the rusty taste of blood where she'd bitten down too hard. Had she really expected him to make a declaration of love?

She'd known from the first Dario wasn't for her. Stupidly she'd let her emotions blind her to that. The surging pain that cramped her stomach and tore at her throat was testimony to the danger of false hope.

Her feelings for him were so different now she knew the real Dario. But, though he knew her too, he still viewed her as nothing more than a convenience. Pain scored her heart. Had he any idea how he hurt her?

'I fit your lifestyle.' Her voice was a rasp of anguish. 'You mean we're good in bed.'

Those broad shoulders lifted in a fluid shrug and his smile tugged at her belly as he leaned close over the desk. 'That goes without saying, *tesoro*. The passion between us is out of this world.'

His satisfied smirk reminded her that while she'd made love he'd had sex. Last night heaven and earth had moved and her soul had soared as she gave herself to the man she loved. But he'd simply craved oblivion after the wrenching memory of past grief. For him it had been a physical and mental catharsis, no more. She'd known it then and she knew it now. That didn't make it easier to stomach.

She'd given herself willingly. Her heart had ached for the vulnerable boy he'd been and the driven man he'd become. But now the pain was for her foolish dreams, the impossible yearning for a man who could never return her feelings. Staying with him to be used in that way would destroy her. She might even begin to hate him.

'Was there anything else?'

His eyes widened at her abrupt tone. 'Of course.'

His brows arrowed down as if he was puzzled by her lack of excitement. Dully she supposed women were usually more enthusiastic about Dario's propositions. Her knees wobbled as she remembered how enthusiastic she'd been just hours ago. The ache of unshed tears filled her mouth.

'I can give you everything, Alissa. Jewels, money, luxury holidays. You'll never have to work again. You'll never have to worry about anything. I'll take care of you.'

'Like a kept woman?' He still thought she cared about those material things? How little he understood her. It wasn't his wealth she craved. It was *him*: obstinate, gorgeous, passionate and challenging.

'No! Like my *wife*.' His tone made it clear this was the highest possible honour. 'You want children. I've seen the way you are with the little ones. You'll make a marvellous mother.' His voice dropped an octave and a thrill of delight ripped through her. 'I want to start a family, Alissa. Soon.' His eyes darkened in promise. 'If you agree we could start trying straight away. Today.'

Alissa trembled at the temptation of his words. He had an unerring ability to find her weak spots. An image filled her mind of Dario on the beach with a little dark-haired tot. Their child.

She sucked in a breath of dismay at how badly she craved the future he painted. Almost enough to forget he'd never love her. Or that he wasn't interested in *their* children, his and hers. She saw it with a sickening clarity that wrenched her heart. He wanted babies to replace the family he'd lost. This was part of his plan to restore the Parisi clan.

'Any woman could give you a baby, Dario. It doesn't have to be me.' Yet she wanted it to be her. Wanted it desperately.

'It's *you* I'm asking, Alissa. Doesn't that mean anything?' He strode round the desk so there was no barrier between them. This close she felt the inevitable desire to nestle in his arms and give him whatever he wanted.

'It's not enough.' She forced the words through stiff lips. It was the hardest thing she'd ever said.

'What?' The single syllable boomed in her ears. He drew himself up to his full, imposing height and stared down his long, perfect, aristocratic nose at her. 'What more do you want? I offer you my name, my honour. I promise you luxury, a life of comfort and ease. The children I know you want.' He scowled.

'Is there nothing else, Dario? No other reason to remain married?'

He was silent so long Alissa couldn't repress a rising bubble of hope. Was it possible he loved her? That he just couldn't say the words? She remembered how he'd cut himself off from emotion, converting his loss and pain into a drive to succeed and an aloofness that set him apart from everyone. Could it be…?

Slowly he nodded, his expression reluctant. She waited, rigid with expectation.

'You must know I feel responsible.' He paused, breathing heavily through flared nostrils. His gaze was brilliant, pinioning hers. 'I misjudged you. I pressured you. I forced you to give me your virginity and—'

'No!' She stumbled back, a palm to her racing heart. She didn't want to hear she should marry him because of some antiquated nonsense about him soiling her 'innocence'. If his strongest feeling for her was guilt, what sort of marriage would it be? Her heart plummeted, her hopes splintered into fragments. 'Don't say any more.'

He closed the gap between them. His scent, his heat, his presence undermined her resolve to remain aloof.

'We're good together,' he purred in the bedroom voice that made her traitorous body tingle even now. 'Admit it, Alissa. You want me as much as I want you.'

He lifted a hand and she jerked back. 'No!' She summoned all the defiance she could muster and glared into his heavy-lidded eyes. 'No,' she said again more quietly. 'I agreed to stay for six months, that's all. I want my freedom when the time's up.'

Dario's face was grim, taut skin over jutting bone. Slashing frown lines scarred his forehead and bracketed his mouth. Defiantly she met his eyes. She read doubt there and determination too. Dario wasn't the sort to give up anything he wanted and right now he wanted her. The irony of it appalled her.

'You're lying,' he murmured, eyes narrowing. 'I know you want me. Your body tells me so.' He wrapped an arm around her, hauled her close and claimed her mouth. His kiss was short and hard. It turned her world upside down and sent desire corkscrewing through her trembling body. Her knees were jelly, her breathing ragged as he pulled back and scrutinised her hot face.

'You can't hide the truth, Alissa. You're mine.'

For one crazy instant she revelled in his proprietorial mastery.

She stumbled back till a wall blocked her escape. 'We're good in bed.' Her voice cracked. 'But I'm sure there's no shortage of women who could satisfy you.' She hid a wince at the idea of Dario with another woman.

He was hers, a silent voice screamed. But Alissa had to stop fooling herself. He could never be hers. Not in the way that counted.

'Once our divorce comes through you can take your pick of women. No doubt you'll find one more suitable than me.' Excruciating pain stabbed her chest as she said it.

'You don't mean that.' There was arrogant certainty in his face. What did she have to do to make him release her?

'I've never been more serious in my life. Staying here would…' Her voice wobbled and she stopped, trying to shore up her defences. She swung round, pretending to stare out the window so he couldn't see the tears brimming.

'You know I never wanted to come here, Dario. You *know* I

didn't want marriage. I was manoeuvred into it. Now you think it's convenient to stay married and you're trying to force me again, telling Donna I'm staying. But I'm not a pawn on a chess board. I'm a woman with thoughts and feelings of my own. I make my own decisions.'

'You believe I'm manipulating you?'

'Aren't you? It feels like it.' Her voice was dull. Pain blunted the sharp edge of her indignation. She wanted to hide somewhere and grieve in peace.

'You believe I'm trying to control you. Like your grandfather did.' His voice seemed to come from a distance. 'That's what you're saying. That I'm like him.'

Miserably she shook her head. Dario and Gianfranco were poles apart. Dario was an honourable, caring man, though proud and blind to love. He stood head and shoulders above scum like her grandfather.

'I just—'

'Stop.' The single word cracked like a gunshot, jerking her to a halt. 'Don't say any more. You've made your feelings abundantly clear.' His voice was as cold and haughty as on the day so long ago when he'd hijacked her wedding. She cringed inside, grateful she couldn't see his face.

'I won't detain you. You can consider our arrangement at an end.' Stupidly she held her breath as if that might stop the pain that lanced her chest. 'There will be a car waiting as soon as you're ready to leave and a ticket on the first flight out.'

Silence. Thick, accusing silence. Then the sound of the door opening and closing as he exited the room.

He'd taken her at her word and left her alone.

It was over.

Alissa drew a raw breath as tears slid down her cheeks and her knees crumpled. She huddled on the floor as grief engulfed her.

She had her freedom.

It was a hollow victory.

* * *

Half an hour later she sat on the wide back seat of the limousine as it purred along the coast road.

Through a glaze of tears she saw the forbidding outline of Castello Parisi on the next headland. It mocked her. It would be here, a permanent part of Dario's life long after he'd forgotten her.

The past had triumphed. She'd met her match in a crumbling pile of ancient masonry.

It was only after they'd passed it that Alissa's numbed brain began to function. Shock clawed her as she realised what Dario had done. He'd sent her away before they'd been married six months. They couldn't inherit the *castello*.

He'd deprived himself of his one chance to acquire the prize he'd worked all his life to win.

CHAPTER FIFTEEN

DARIO stood on the beach, hands jammed in his pockets, staring at the restless sea. It reminded him of Alissa, the way her eyes danced with pleasure, her quicksilver quality, the energy she brought to everyday living. The passion she'd bestowed on him.

His chest constricted at the idea of never seeing her again. Never holding her or watching her eyes light with passion. Never sharing those silent moments when the world faded and there were just the two of them, connected by a force so strong it defied everything he'd ever known.

He'd fooled himself into hoping she felt it too, the well-spring of emotion and need that drew him to her. It had been a false hope.

A tide of despair swamped him.

She'd broken the seals on emotions he'd buried a lifetime ago. Emotions he'd forgotten and new feelings he'd never before experienced.

If he hadn't met Alissa he'd still be that remote, diffident man, isolated by pride and lack of emotion.

She'd left him raw and wounded, horrified by the man she'd revealed. Her absolute refusal to countenance a permanent relationship forced him to take stock of who he was. It wasn't a pretty sight.

He'd treated her like a whore, demanding she sleep with him for payment. He'd stolen her virginity then not had the decency to release her. He'd used her to sate his lust, regardless of her own needs. He hadn't stopped to find out what she wanted, had just assumed what they had was as good for her as it was for him.

He'd learned nothing. In the end he'd been so desperate to keep her he'd tried to bulldoze her into staying. Manipulate her into agreeing. She, who'd fought most of her life against her domineering grandfather.

His shoulders slumped as the truth pummelled him, like waves on a high sea.

He had nothing to offer her. All he had was his quest to recoup past glories. But now he understood no wealth, power or prestige could make up for the emptiness inside him. The emptiness now she had gone.

She'd been right to leave. Yet already he found himself planning to follow and fight for her. He had no notion how he'd convince her to return, no leverage he could use, but he *couldn't* give up. He—

'Dario.'

Hairs prickled his nape as he imagined her voice on the surging waves. By now she'd be halfway to the airport, eager to be gone.

He should give her time before he pursued her, time for her righteous anger to abate. Time for him to develop a plan. But his desperation was too great. He spun round and almost slammed into the figure blocking the path to the villa.

'Alissa.'

Was that his voice? That raw, hungry gasp? He was beyond caring how much that revealed. He cared only that she was here.

Her hands were small, capable and *real* in his grasp. He felt her warmth, looked down into her cornflower-blue eyes and still couldn't believe. *She was here.*

It was all he could do not to drag her into his arms and kiss her doubts away, blotting out the world.

But that hadn't worked before. He had to make this work between them. There was no other alternative.

'Dario.' His name tasted perfect on her lips. She wanted him to tug her close and kiss her doubts and questions away, take her to that special place they alone shared. But he held back.

Suddenly her idea seemed too crazy even for words. Had she made a terrible mistake? She shivered as ice covered her heart. Her tongue froze as she looked up into his set features.

'I came back because I realised…'

'Yes?' His tone gave nothing away. Only the hammering pulse at the base of his throat gave her hope. That and his grip, tight enough to make her blood pulse hard and slow in her fingers.

But he had himself in hand. Dario Parisi, careful and in control. His expression was unreadable.

She hesitated, hearing her blood pound in her ears. She was afraid to lay herself bare but she had to know. She couldn't leave him while there was even the remotest possibility…

'I realised you wouldn't get the *castello* if I left.'

His iron-hard grip on her fingers slackened and her hands slipped free, falling to her sides.

'You came back because of the *castello*?'

His eyes turned gun-metal grey, blank and devoid of light. The sight doused her last hope. Suddenly she wished she was in the limo, cocooned from everything by the tinted glass that concealed her misery.

She'd made an awful mistake. The realisation numbed her brain.

'I said you were free to go. I do not hold you to our agreement. I forced you into that bargain unfairly. I won't do it again.'

He raised a hand to spear through his sleek, perfect hair. Was it imagination or did his fingers tremble?

'But you need the *castello*. I understand what it means to you.' She paused, horrified to realise how badly she wanted to stay. If acquiring the place would bring him peace after a lifetime of pain she was prepared to swallow her pride and help him. And it would give her a few more precious weeks with him. 'It's only for a short while. I could move into a guest room and...'

'No! It's impossible. Do not even suggest it.'

Alissa's eyes prickled and her throat jammed as roiling emotion engulfed her. He wouldn't even let her help him achieve his dream. She really had destroyed whatever affection he'd had for her. Desperately she told herself it was for the best. She swung round to leave.

'Alissa.' His voice stopped her. It wasn't a command but a hoarse plea. 'Please understand that I will not dishonour you any more.'

Dishonour! What did she care for honour when her heart was breaking? The blue Sicilian sky dimmed as despair pressed down on her. She lifted one leaden foot to walk away.

'If you had come back for any reason but the *castello*...'

She stumbled and strong arms wrapped round her before she could find her feet. Dario hauled her back against him and she shut her eyes at the exquisite sensation of their bodies locked together.

To be held by the man she loved, feel his heart beating behind her, his arms like warm steel, supporting her...

It was delicious torture, pleasure so poignant her poor heart welled and overflowed.

'But the *castello* means everything to you,' she whispered when at last she found her voice.

'You're wrong, *tesoro*.' His words were muffled in her hair as he nuzzled her scalp. Tremors of reaction vibrated through her and she arched back against him. 'Once it did. But not now, not for a long time. Not since I fell in love.'

Alissa heard the words but couldn't take them in. He can't have said—

She turned so swiftly she bumped her nose on his chin. She tried to back away to see his expression but his arms locked relentlessly round her. He hauled her close and she heard the thunder of his heart pound against her, matching her own galloping pulse.

'The *castello* is just a place.' His voice rumbled up from deep in his chest. She felt every word. 'A special place, but not nearly as important to me as you, *carissima*. That's why I had to let you go. It isn't worth the pain you were suffering, being here with me. I've abided by my promise to my father, but he wouldn't expect me to destroy the woman I adore to get it.'

'You love me?' Had he really said it?

'I love you, Alissa. I've never known anything like this feeling.' He grasped her hand and pressed it to his heart. The pulse of his life force beneath her palm, his words a hot caress against her forehead, made the unbelievable real. Excitement sheared through her.

'For months I told myself it was lust, but from the first it was far more. You are such a woman, *my* sort of woman. Strong, independent, but caring and gentle.'

He put his hands on her shoulders and stepped back till at last she could see his face. His silvery eyes shone overbright. She'd never seen that expression before, of joy and fear mixed together. Hope sang in her breast.

'Dario.' Her voice was choked as she reached up to cup his jaw. 'I can't believe it. You're so—'

'Stubborn? Unwilling to see what's under my nose?'

'Of course not.' A smile broke on her lips as she met his eyes and saw the tenderness there. An expression of love so real, so honest, for a moment words were beyond her. 'I never guessed. You never hinted…'

'That's because I didn't know myself till I'd sent you away.' He turned his face into her palm and pressed feverish kisses there, sending her body into meltdown. 'I thought it was my pride you'd injured, till I realised the truth. I'd become like the man I hated most in the world. I'd become as ruthless as he, desperate to get what I wanted no matter what the cost. When I saw how deeply I'd hurt you I knew I'd do anything to make it better, even let you go.'

Regret shimmered in his eyes. An agony of self-hate that evoked all her protective instincts.

'Shh, Dario. You're not like him at all. You could never be. You're honourable and generous. You genuinely care.' She drew a shaky breath and bared her soul. 'I love you too. But I thought you'd never feel the same. That's why I had to leave—'

His plundering mouth stopped her confession. He snagged her close and tilted her head to accommodate his sweet invasion. It was all there in his kiss, the heady emotion, the shared passion, the trust and promise for the future. Everything she'd ever dreamt of. And more.

'Tell me again,' he whispered against her lips. Heaven was in his hoarse command. In the way he held her, as if she was the most precious treasure in all the world.

'I love you, Dario. I'd trust you with my life.'

He crushed her so close she could barely breathe, yet she smiled as she looked up into the earnest features of the man she adored. He was as handsome as ever. But never had he looked so gorgeous as now, with love shining clear and bright in his eyes.

'*Bella* Alissa. Will you marry me? A proper wedding this time. In a church with all your friends and family. A wedding with all the trimmings and a reception in the town square for everyone to join in.' His voice resonated with the depth of his feelings. 'I want everyone to hear when I promise to love and honour my darling wife.'

Alissa knew no hesitation at all as she leaned close and murmured, 'Yes, Dario. I will.'

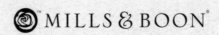

FREE

2 BOOKS AND A SURPRISE GIFT!

We would like to take this opportunity to thank you for reading this Mills & Boon® book by offering you the chance to take TWO more specially selected titles from the Modern™ series absolutely FREE! We're also making this offer to introduce you to the benefits of the Mills & Boon® Book Club™—

- ★ **FREE home delivery**
- ★ **FREE gifts and competitions**
- ★ **FREE monthly Newsletter**
- ★ **Books available before they're in the shops**
- ★ **Exclusive Mills & Boon Book Club offers**

Accepting these FREE books and gift places you under no obligation to buy; you may cancel at any time, even after receiving your free shipment. Simply complete your details below and return the entire page to the address below. You don't even need a stamp!

YES! Please send me 2 free Modern books and a surprise gift. I understand that unless you hear from me, I will receive 4 superb new titles every month for just £3.19 each, postage and packing free. I am under no obligation to purchase any books and may cancel my subscription at any time. The free books and gift will be mine to keep in any case.

P9ZEE

Ms/Mrs/Miss/Mr...Initials ....

BLOCK CAPITALS PLEASE

Surname ....

Address ....

....

....Postcode ....

Send this whole page to:
The Mills & Boon Book Club, FREEPOST CN81, Croydon, CR9 3WZ